THE RULES OF ENGAGEMENT

ALSO BY THE AUTHOR

NON-FICTION

Unto the Skies: A Biography of Amy Johnson
(Book Guild, 2017)

THE RULES OF ENGAGEMENT

K. A. Lalani

The Book Guild Ltd

First published in Great Britain in 2019 by
The Book Guild Ltd
9 Priory Business Park
Wistow Road, Kibworth
Leicestershire, LE8 0RX
Freephone: 0800 999 2982
www.bookguild.co.uk
Email: info@bookguild.co.uk
Twitter: @bookguild

Typeset in Aldine401 BT

Printed and bound in Great Britain by 4edge Limited

ISBN 978 1912881 024

British Library Cataloguing in Publication Data.
A catalogue record for this book is available from the British Library.

Printed on FSC accredited paper

I dedicate this novel to the memory of those who fought in the
First World War and who made the ultimate sacrifice.
"Lest we forget that for our tomorrow, they gave their today."

PRELUDE

Ashburn Park, Dorset – June 28, 1914

Stephen Trentham stood at the window of his suite at Ashburn Park. He loved the rambling old house with its ivy-covered sandstone walls in which he had grown up, the second son of the second son, a fact which had enabled him to realise early in life that there was little prospect of him inheriting the Trentham estate, and to get over any residual disappointment he might have felt with the situation. In contrast to his friend and weekend guest, Daniel, the Viscount Swiffen, who would inherit an earldom. Seeing him suddenly, sauntering towards the house through the shimmering heat haze of a scorching summer day caused Stephen to smile, raising his hand in greeting. Daniel smiled in response, Stephen realised quickly however, that it wasn't him Daniel was smiling at, as he approached the house over the brow of the sloping verdant grounds, which undulated down to the sea. The figure attracting Daniel's attention and earning the smile which lit his face was his cousin, Olivia Trentham. She came to greet Daniel, her hands outstretched and he took them with a gentle squeeze.

Stephen watched the scene being played out below him with a sense of unease. He held a deep affection for his cousin, wanting to see her happy. He also had an abiding respect for

Daniel, and having stayed on numerous occasions at *Javrons,* the sprawling estate in Hertfordshire, he could see why a potential attachment would be attractive to Olivia, but Stephen held firm to his misgivings. Although surprised that he had leapt to such a conclusion so swiftly, the spontaneous warmth of their greeting suggested they had got to know one another very well since their first lunch meeting, which he had also attended. Although he was interested to learn how frequently they were meeting to become as close as they now appeared, which of them was spurring the affection and providing the impetus for their burgeoning friendship he wasn't sure, but was determined to find out. The colour bleaching from his face as he contemplated all the possibilities now vying for consideration in his mind, because few people knew Daniel as well as he, and with that came the instinct that Daniel was wrong for Olivia, which *he* couldn't ignore.

Confronting his friend on this subject was the *only* option. Turning away from the window, Stephen knew that to save his cousin from potential heartache later, any blossoming romance with Daniel should be discouraged. He had turned from the window the moment Daniel looked up to acknowledge him, a smile lighting his vivid blue eyes. Many of their peers at Eton and then at Oxford tended to dismiss Daniel as being overly vain and *effete.* He, however, believed his friend was resilient, possessing a strong inner core that many in their circle tended to overlook, but that fact notwithstanding, he had still felt the need to protect Daniel from his *proclivities* throughout that time. He felt a *frisson* of something now, but was reluctant to give a name to it, suffice to say that had he known what was in his friend's mind, he would have *erred* on inviting him as his guest. He had to – albeit reluctantly – compliment them on their discretion. The fact that his uncle Edgar, a senior partner in the publishing house *Trentham & Westmacott,* was currently negotiating a contract which would lead to Daniel being launched into literary circles with his first volume of poetry, was the obvious route through which they had been developing their friendship. He knew that Olivia, although not employed by the firm, liked making the acquaintance of promising young literary talent who caught her father's attention.

Stephen glanced at his watch, frowning slightly; the plan was to leave for London after lunch so the timing of his intervention was *crucial*. He shivered slightly despite the heat of the day, because what he was contemplating gave him no pleasure. Blood ties were important though he decided, sighing heavily. This most mundane of Sundays was swiftly developing into something momentous for reasons that he couldn't have foreseen; by the day's end just how momentous it was became clearer, as events in a distant city on the underbelly of Europe became a catalyst for all that was to follow.

Covington, Devonshire – June 28, 1914

Alex Conyer felt a lightness of heart boarding the Great Western train bound for Exeter which would take him the short trip to Covington.

Sitting in the dusty carriage, his widow's peak of blond hair partially shielding his eyes from the glare of the sun, he tugged the dusty green blind, checking the watch he had been bequeathed by his maternal grandfather. Seeing the midday hour approach his spirits soared. Sunday meant he spent most of the day with Laura. He was usually invited to join them for Sunday lunch, the preparation of which consumed most of her morning after attendance at church. Today he planned on taking Laura for a long stroll after lunch, while her father, George Weston, the station master, dozed idly for an hour or so then read the papers, as there were no services stopping at Covington upon the Sabbath until four in the afternoon.

Alex knew he wanted to make his future with Laura and he believed she felt the same, although some doubt occasionally assailed him as Laura tended to believe her future remained in the sleepy backwater of Covington, while he wanted them to broaden their horizons.

He had lost count of the occasions she had gently *urged* caution on him, in tones filled with affection, not to get too carried away with *his* plans for their future. Although he had a valuable ally in her widowed father who actively encouraged his only child to follow her heart, even if that meant him losing her. It was the natural order of things he said, despite her nodding at him dismissively. In quiet moments, however, he assured Alex he would keep working on her, an assurance that caused Alex to smile as the train pulled into Covington. He stood to wave at Laura standing at the window of the station master's cottage in which she had been born eighteen years earlier. She smiled back, wiping the perspiration from her forehead with the back of her hand. Her moss-green eyes dancing merrily at the sight of him. Alex pushed down the window and was about to alight, his mood darkening suddenly; as he caught sight of the head porter, Charlie Stoughton. He was three years Alex's senior and an unapologetic bully. Stoughton was about to say something condescending in his generally oafish manner, until another alighting passenger signalled to him for assistance. In that moment as passengers mingled on the platform, Alex stepped down to find Laura running into his arms.

Alex Conyer had been her *beau* for a time that seemed like forever. Her love for him growing deeper with the years. Wrapping her arms around his neck, she welcomed the passionate kiss he seared onto her lips. Stoughton watched the scene playing out with a characteristic sneer, as a couple of suited young men whistled encouragingly, one of them slapping Alex good naturedly on the shoulder. They boarded the Exeter-bound train as it meandered out of Covington, gaining speed as it disappeared from view.

Sarajevo, Bosnia – June 28, 1914

There was a distinct sense of dissent in the atmosphere but it was muffled by the enthusiastic cheering of those sufficiently imbued by the lure of power, and those considered *too* feeble and subservient not to come out and welcome the Archduke Franz Ferdinand and his wife Sophie to this far-flung colony of the Hapsburg Empire.

The young Serbian Nationalist student looked furtively around him, trying to gauge the general mood of the crowd in whose proximity he had chosen to stand. He felt no obligation to welcome the heir to the Hapsburg throne to *his* city. Deference had no impact on him. He was conscious of a more febrile atmosphere which he would have liked to encourage had he believed it safe. He was convinced the air of celebration he could hear was just an illusion. There was still sufficient ill-feeling towards the Governor-general, specifically for the autocratic rule of law that he had imposed upon the people of Sarajevo, and to have chosen today of all days for the Archduke's tour of the city, on an anniversary *so* significant to the history of the Bosnian people was especially *crass* and insensitive.

If the plans that he and his comrades had put in place were successful then very soon the Hapsburg rulers would have it confirmed, despite the outward display of jubilation by those too cowed to know any better, the extent to which the people of Bosnia resented the Archduke's presence as they chafed against the suffocating restrictive nature of *his* rule.

Gavrilo Princip smiled, standing amid the gathering crowd outside the Moritz Schiller café, which was being held back from the wide boulevard of Appel Quay. The plan was for him to remain there incognito, soaking up the atmosphere, waiting for the moment for which they had planned so meticulously. Although welcoming the dignitaries was *abhorrent* to him, he had betrayed no sense of his outrage. In the shimmering heat-haze of a June day, the motorcade approached.

Gavrilo felt his palms perspiring as he gripped the handle of the revolver he had concealed. The crowd around him continued cheering, but he had grown immune to their misplaced sense of loyalty. As the motorcade was almost upon them outside the café, the chauffeur's nerve seemed to desert him, sensing perhaps that another attempt was to made upon the Archduke's life following the grenade which had earlier fallen into the canopy at the back of their car; that it had not been the random act of a lone assassin but the first sortie in an organised attack. It was too late for the chauffeur to reverse down Appel Quay and in that moment Gavrilo realised *his* moment had come. Stepping out from the crowd he raised his Browning revolver and, aiming it at the Archduke, he fired his first shot, hitting Archduke Franz Ferdinand in the neck, severing his jugular vein. The colour began draining from his face and as he whispered to Duchess Sophie that *"it was nothing."* Blood began pouring from his mouth as Gavrilo fired a second shot, which was intended for the Governor-general but it ricocheted, hitting the Duchess Sophie instead. As confusion reigned, police officers descended upon Gavrilo, forcing him to the ground and seizing his Browning revolver, while his cyanide capsule failed to make him the *martyr* he had hoped to become. As the red stain on the grey and yellow tunic spread, it became evident that the Archduke was haemorrhaging rapidly, his life force ebbing away. The bullet to his jugular vein had been a fatal shot and he was effectively dead within seconds. His beloved wife, the Duchess Sophie, was also killed by the shot which hit her. A deep sense of shock reverberated throughout the crowd. The cheering ceased, and the silence which followed it was swiftly replaced with anguished sobs, mixed with gasps of horror at the carnage they had witnessed, recoiling from the fact that it had been committed by a young man who had been standing among them only moments before.

As the grim reality of it began to take hold, seeping into the collective conscience, that a Serbian Nationalist had committed this heinous crime and that the Hapsburg rulers, robbed of their heir, would *demand* their retribution.

As telegraph wires fizzed across the continent, relaying news of the horror Sarajevo had played host to, the enormous impact of it, began to unfold.

1

Stephen waited patiently in his suite for Daniel, growing increasingly frustrated when he failed to appear. They had decided not to join the rest of the family at church, but Stephen expected Olivia would have gone, quickly realising however, after a swift exchange with a footman, that Olivia had decided instead to accept Daniel's invitation to go for a walk.

So as the midday hour approached Stephen grew weary, doubting he would get an opportunity to discuss the situation with Daniel before lunch. Finishing his coffee in a gulp, he made his way downstairs.

He was still inclined to give his friend the opportunity to divulge the depth of his friendship with Olivia in private, but felt he had the right to *demand* assurance from Daniel as he had issued the invitation to join them for the weekend. As he descended into the oak panelled Grand Hall of Ashburn Park, which although very imposing had no comparison to the splendour of *Javrons*, Stephen glanced at his watch, his attention suddenly diverted towards Olivia, laughing gaily as she entered the hall on Daniel's arm.

'Morning Stephen. How are you?'

'I'm very well, thank you Olivia. If you could give me a moment with Daniel?'

Olivia smiled, raising a quizzical eyebrow at her cousin, she glanced back at Daniel. 'Sounds intriguing. I shall leave you to it.'

Stephen had tried to keep his tone neutral, but he was concerned that his growing frustration might have betrayed him. Daniel's smile faded slightly. 'Sounds ominous Stephen! Have I incurred your wrath?'

Olivia laughed again. 'Surely not! Although I hope I haven't been monopolising his time.'

'Not at all. Although I am surprised you both appear so well acquainted?'

'That is because Olivia has been kind enough to join her father and myself for lunch on several occasions, during which she has proved herself invaluable with ideas about my forthcoming volume of poetry. She has become – I think it's no exaggeration to state – an *inspiration*, to the extent that she is swiftly becoming my latest *muse*.'

As Stephen led them towards the library, he couldn't help wondering which of them wanted this blossoming friendship to grow in the manner that it appeared to be doing, but he suspected it was Daniel so reinforcing his initial reaction, and making him now more determined to confront his friend on the issue. Stephen closed the library door as Daniel made his way in, noticing how Olivia looked slightly askance at him, shaking her head as she went upstairs.

'You sound so earnest Stephen that I cannot help but wonder if I have been less than worthy of your hospitality?' Stephen smiled politely. This was Daniel at his most *insufferable*. Overtly aristocratic and patrician. It was at moments such as this that he stretched the elasticity of their friendship to its limit.

'You have in a manner of speaking. I saw you earlier approaching Olivia over the brow of the hill. I waved to you from my suite but you didn't notice me, you were so focused on my cousin. Taking her hand in the manner of a lover, or a betrothed, which cannot be of course. Aside from the fact you barely know one another, there's the fact Olivia cannot provide you with what you *need,* and what I expect she most desires.' Daniel stood aside the hearth, his elbow resting indolently on the mantelpiece. His vivid blue eyes dancing with barely concealed mischief, some would say devilment, but Stephen was unimpressed. He had seen that look before and he knew it usually spelt trouble.

'On the contrary my friend. Your delightful cousin can provide me with exactly what *I* need. What the Old Man – sorry, my father – the current Earl demands from me. An heir!'

'This isn't a joke Daniel.'

Daniel smiled, shaking his head. 'Believe me Stephen I can see from the stiffness of your demeanour that you're not in the mood for mirth, and I am serious. Although Olivia and I haven't reached any sort of understanding, we have grown increasingly fond of each other.'

'I can see that,' Stephen stated flatly.

'With evident disapproval I suspect.'

'With genuine *concern* Daniel. How can I possibly not approve? We have been friends for years. One day you *will* become the Earl of Royston. I have seen your family estate, stayed there as your guest. How could Olivia's head not be turned by *Javrons* and the potential of all that it represents. So my concern *is* for you both!' Stephen didn't need to say aloud what they were both thinking, but he continued. 'She would be so *hurt,* devastated – if…'

'Ah, if I were to succumb to my notorious *proclivities* – as I believe you like to refer to them?'

Stephen was struggling to control his temper. He thought he might actually *loathe* his friend at that moment and the frivolity with which he was treating Olivia's feelings – unless – and he dismissed the idea almost immediately, they weren't actually as serious about each other as he had imagined.

'I protected you from yourself more than once first at Eton and then…'

Daniel approached Stephen tentatively, unsure of his friend's mood. He nodded slowly, his smile reduced in an effort to look serious. 'I'm grateful truly. You've always had my back.'

'Even when you couldn't always appreciate my interventions at the time,' Stephen added soberly.

'Even then. I have lost count of the occasions you have saved me and the Swiffen name from untold embarrassment.'

Stephen was about to speak, until Daniel put a restraining hand on his shoulder and this time his smile held only sincerity. The patrician arrogance that Daniel knew he resented had been replaced by warmth. 'In the end – my obligations to the earldom aside – I can only bring shame to the Swiffen name by being myself. Have you gone to all this effort over the years, just to leave me to my own devices now, knowing the likely consequences? Our old adversaries from Eton, Crowley and Frobisher are *longing* for the day I publicly disgrace myself.'

Stephen nodded. Daniel was right. From the moment they had become friends at Eton he had assumed the role of Daniel's protector. Although his friend's conduct frequently made him his own worst enemy. There was, however, so much more at stake than the Swiffen reputation and Daniel's well-being. Whatever it was that Daniel and Olivia now appeared to have may lead to nothing. Daniel would still find a wife, an arrangement would be made for the purpose of producing a Swiffen heir. His concerns, however genuine at this moment, could prove groundless.

'I need the respectability of marriage. I'll admit the thought petrifies me, but it's the absolute imperative for me to inherit in the manner my father expects.'

Daniel placed his palms against Stephen's cheeks, whispering, 'Thank you,' into his ear, but for what Stephen wasn't sure.

For him, nothing had been resolved by this conversation, and he'd had a plan of action fixed in his mind. The instinct to protect Olivia uppermost, but he felt as constrained as before by a conflict of duties. If his cousin was to become the next Countess Swiffen, could she enjoy true happiness amid the gilded splendour of her existence, and could Daniel ever stop being himself, never tempted to surrender to the *proclivities*, of which they had so often referred, even with the cover that a good marriage provided him?

As Daniel retreated, Stephen smiled softly, but inside he was writhen with doubt. 'So you would be prepared to subject my cousin to the heartache she would inevitably suffer were you to become betrothed? Struggling to resist succumbing to how you truly felt!'

Daniel looked away. He had grown genuinely fond of Olivia Trentham but he couldn't claim to be in love with her. So in that respect Stephen was entitled to be concerned. Whether Olivia was falling for him he couldn't be sure, as it wasn't something he had previously experienced. He was certain that every young debutante, whether a sister or a cousin within their circle, would be discreetly discouraged against him in the respect of a romantic liaison years ago. As much he was aware it was the title and the *Javrons* estate that provided his marketable value to any potential bride.

'Not intentionally. I could never do that to her. I know that by hurting Olivia I would be getting at you. I'm not even convinced her feelings for me are that strong. You evidently feel differently, having raised your concerns. Honestly though, do you think Edgar would give his blessing to such a match? From what I know of his politics he is strictly adverse to the life that I have been born to lead. Would he realistically want that for his only child?'

Stephen inclined his head. Daniel had a point. Edgar liked Daniel but privately he disapproved on principal of the hereditary system. Understandably given some of the opposition the Asquith Government had faced from Conservative peers in the House of Lords for its social reforms.

'If he knew it would make Olivia happy, then yes, I think he could give you his blessing, albeit with some reservation. My uncle is a pragmatist.'

'While Olivia is a romanticist at heart. So there is a definitive conflict,' Daniel responded light heartedly, to which Stephen smiled. They had respectfully acknowledged the other's position, but aside from that Stephen was inclined to believe he may have overplayed his hand, although he remained convinced his cousin could easily fall for Daniel's charms and believe herself to be in love with him. Knowing her as he did, she would want to pursue that to its natural conclusion, even if it were to be marriage.

Daniel embraced Stephen warmly and for a brief moment he felt as if his friend had felt a *frisson,* but the moment passed, and he pulled away. Stephen had urged him many times to learn from his mistakes, and yet his impetuous nature never afforded him the opportunity to pull back. He sometimes wondered if his family knew, and that it was an unspoken knowledge that would remain thus, for fear that by giving voice to it would leave them vulnerable, exposed to the very dangers Stephen had so valiantly protected him from. For his father, reputation was everything. The continuation of the Swiffen name and the earldom were paramount. No personal motive or desire could ever come before that. That was the burden of responsibility his father had accepted and so it would pass to him. His parents he knew had married for duty. Affection, if it could be attained, was a secondary consideration, and with it respect would come later. For him the possibility was especially acute that he *might* be living a lie, that he reflected was the destiny, he had reconciled himself to for as long as he could remember.

Alex Conyer lay on his back gazing up at a cloudless sky. Intense heat had permeated everything today. He stretched out his hand so that his fingers were touching Laura's. It sent a frisson of delight through him just having physical contact with her. In many respects it would be hard to leave this idyllic corner of Devonshire, but he was conscious that it was idyllic because it was all they knew. The boundary of their world and the limit of their life experience. London was such a world away to them to the extent that it might well have been as close as Paris or New York.

Covington was only a tiny backwater in the county of Devonshire, and yet it comprised all they needed, or so Laura believed, as she was often inclined to tell him, but she could count the times she had ventured as far as Exeter on the fingers of one hand. He *felt* differently. He didn't want this town, as charming as it was to the countless visitors who flocked here during the summer, to be all there was for them.

Leaving Covington, her father and all the happy memories it held would be harder for Laura, but he felt constrained by the ties that bound her here, because he *needed* to be close to her. He felt no such ties binding him to Covington, but he couldn't contemplate leaving her behind, exposed to the attention of the oafish head porter, Stoughton, whose lascivious interest repulsed her. 'He makes my skin crawl every time he comes near me,' she was frequently inclined to say. 'Even his presence puts me on my guard'

Alex couldn't understand why they had to tolerate Stoughton until Laura's father had explained that he was an employee of Great Western Railway who had been transferred to Covington because there had been some trouble at his previous station. Probably involving another girl Alex had surmised, as he saw Stoughton's biggest problem that *he* deluded himself into thinking he was irresistible.

He rolled on the grass so that his body touched Laura, luxuriating in the sensation of proximity. He felt the warmth of her body against his, and he chafed at the sexual longing he had for her against her insistence that they should wait. Laura looked at him, the smile lighting her moss-green eyes. He kissed her hard, feeling the fervour as she kissed him back. His widow's peak fell across his eyes, and he pushed it away, his right hand resting on the curve of her hip. He kissed her again with more urgency as his hand began a journey upwards towards the swell of her breasts, but she gently pushed it away.

Sitting up she glanced at the gold watch, his most valuable possession from his grandfather who had been a stoker on the Great Western Railway. She smiled, 'Soon but not yet.'

Alex sighed heavily, and falling back he gazed up at the sky. Sundays were always too short, however much of the day he spent with Laura. Tomorrow would bring the drudging formality of his job as a typesetter on the *Covington Echo*. There was a mundane uniformity to his life between Monday and Saturday mornings which he found intensely stifling, regardless of how much time he managed to spend with her. This provided him with the impetus to strive for something more for them beyond the limited confines of Covington. He knew Laura could settle for remaining here and be content with that decision. He was certain, however, that to realise his potential he had to move away to seek the best version of himself that he could be. The dilemma he faced was would he regret forever sacrificing his dream by deciding, for Laura's sake, to stay.

2

The impact of what had taken place in Sarajevo that Sunday morning took time to have its impact on the public, however, Stephen Trentham was mildly aware, although still too troubled by personal matters to fully absorb its potential ramifications when he returned to London that evening.

The sun, a burning orange orb, was dipping towards sunset; when he alighted a taxi outside his flat on Charles Street, Daniel having left him to finish the journey alone, upon arrival at the Swiffen town house on Cavendish Square.

They had, along with Edgar and Olivia, taken the train from Dorset shortly after lunch, which had been a tense affair. Olivia had been her usual engaging self, although curious about what had kept Stephen and Daniel talking for so long in the library earlier, her efforts in that regard, however, had earned her precious little. One of his other cousins, fifteen year-old Matthew, had been in a typically combative mood, challenging Daniel about his intentions towards Olivia. Daniel was taking it in good spirits until Charles Trentham assailed him with an uncharacteristic burst of temper, which left a pall of unease for the remainder of the meal.

Charles Trentham, whose demeanour had always been considerably less relaxed and urbane than his youngest brother, had insisted on speaking to Stephen privately before they left, in which he told his nephew he had felt *coerced* into accepting Daniel as a weekend guest. It was a confrontation Stephen had still found – although not untypical of Charles's attitude –mildly insulting.

'I am not inclined to justify my feelings, nor do I comprehend the nature of your friendship with this man, but I cannot see how my brother Edgar can appear *so* relaxed about Olivia's burgeoning relationship with him. She is evidently smitten. I would appreciate it therefore if you would refrain from issuing him another invitation to spend the weekend at Ashburn.'

'I seriously doubt given the way Matthew spoke to him during lunch that Daniel will be inclined to accept another invitation, although I issued it myself based on the numerous occasions that I have been a guest of the Earl Royston. Daniel was as much Edgar and Olivia's guest this weekend as he was mine.'

Charles was seething at this point, using every ounce of self-control he possessed to restrain himself from another outburst. 'Now that you have fulfilled your obligation to reciprocate the invitation, can I ask you not to repeat it?'

'Are you saying my friends are not welcome at Ashburn, Uncle Charles?'

'Don't insult our intelligence Stephen by feigning ignorance of my meaning. I don't approve of the Viscount Swiffen's courtship – if that is what it is developing into – of my niece. While I scarcely believe Edgar could contemplate such a match and I don't intend to encourage it under this roof!'

'I also want only the best for Olivia, but I am intrigued Uncle Charles, that you should feel so strongly that the son of an Earl is such unsuitable husband material.'

At that point Stephen excused himself, before he said something that he would regret; but the confrontation had left him seething, impacting on his demeanour for the remainder of the afternoon. Charles had always been a *bore*. He lacked the finesse of his younger brothers, and although Stephen suspected his father would have struggled to accept Daniel's lifestyle, he couldn't have imagined him being as insufferably rude as Charles had been today. Standing now in his lounge on the third storey of a house offering views towards Berkley Square, Stephen gripped the back of a chair. When the knock came at the door, with the uniformed telegraph boy standing there, Stephen gave him some coins for his trouble, before reading the contents, with a rising sense of foreboding, his brow pleating in a frown. It was as stark as it was succinct:

Assassination in Sarajevo. Stop.

Archduke Ferdinand of Austria dead. Stop. He screwed the telegram into ball, tossing it into an empty grate and sighing heavily, poured himself a Cognac. It was very much earlier than he generally indulged, but it had been a long and trying day. From the moment he had watched Daniel and Olivia meeting in the grounds of Ashburn and embracing so warmly, he should have sensed the awful portents the day was going to present him with. In the morning he would have to confront whatever policy the Foreign Office had towards the skirmish in Sarajevo and likely contend with it. But for now he was still too angry about the sneering insinuation that had laid behind Charles's comments, which he had no doubt appeared to question aspects of his private life – with his continued bachelor status – at the centre of it, to fully comprehend what the potential aftermath of a political assassination in the Balkans might be.

★ ★ ★

Stephen remained ill at ease regarding the events of the weekend when he arrived at the Foreign Office the following morning, however, with news about the assassination in Sarajevo rife,

11

and speculation about what the diplomatic response might be buzzing around, he had no time to dwell on personal matters, deciding to put his shoulder to the wheel in the national crisis now confronting the country. Hitherto the House of Commons had been focusing its attention, and in some cases most of its ire, on the issue of Irish Nationalism, which was of paramount concern to the Asquith Government as it depended on the support of the Irish Nationalist Members of Parliament to secure their Commons majority.

As June slid into July, the complex diplomatic brinkmanship gathered pace, and tensions between the conflicted nations increased.

He heard little from Daniel during this time other than a brief telegram informing him he was remaining in London, issuing two invitations to join him for dinner, both of which Stephen was forced to decline due to pressures of work, leading him to speculate whether Daniel would invite Olivia instead.

As the last week of July approached, and the Commons was due to retire for the summer recess, it appeared that no escalation of hostilities was imminent, although Austria had repeated its demand that Serbia hand over the culprits responsible for the assassination of the Archduke. A demand for which they had full support from Germany, while Serbia continued to rely on Russia's support for their position. Prime Minister Herbert Asquith was privately concerned that despite the current *impasse,* Europe seemed to be heading towards the brink of Armageddon, although officially the Government adhered to its belief that Germany would ultimately pull Austria back from all-out war.

That appeared less likely as the last days of the month approached, and the Asquiths were looking forward to their holiday in Scotland. On July 28, Austria, tiring of Serbia's stalling, formally declared war, and by the first weekend of August Germany and Russia were at war, with Britain struggling to remain on the sidelines. There was cheering and gaiety on the streets which left the Prime Minister baffled. Germany showed no respect for Belgian neutrality, a position that the British Government stated it would not tolerate, issuing Berlin with an ultimatum that unless Belgium's decision to remain neutral was respected, it would be at war with the British Empire. The deadline for Germany to respond was at midnight, Berlin time, on Tuesday 4 August, an hour earlier in London and that night Asquith invited Foreign Secretary Lord Grey and other senior members of the Government to join him in the Cabinet Room. The solemnity of the occasion apparent, Stephen dined with Edgar at his club on Northumberland Avenue. Stephen found his uncle as much as he was in a sombre mood. The personal matter both had set aside had, however, been pushed to the fore by virtue of a letter Charles Trentham had written his brother. When Edgar handed the letter to Stephen he read it through twice, and handing it back he could see that its contents left his uncle seething.

'How dare *he* presume to know what is best for my daughter? I'll admit I have been downplaying the friendship between Olivia and Daniel. Your cousin is a romantic. She forms attachments to several young men she meets, most of which have so far fizzled out. So I had no reason to believe this one would be any different. While Charles attaches a great import to *his* priorities in regard to running Ashburn, he fails to realise that I have more pressing matters to consider. Speaking of which do you still think we can avoid being dragged into conflict?'

Stephen looked down at the Cognac swirling around in his glass. Most of the conversation around the Club tonight, in unusually hushed tones, had inevitably been centred on the prospects of war. He looked at Edgar who smiled thinly.

'Your silence speaks for itself. I can no longer claim to be hopeful – let alone optimistic. It just seems incredible that an assassination in Sarajevo we hadn't even known about as we travelled back from Dorset that weekend can lead to this – an ultimatum tonight that would commit this country to war.'

Edgar shook his head, before continuing, 'Doesn't the Kaiser realise that if he refuses to heed our Government's ultimatum, he will in effect be waging war against his first cousin King George, and the might of the British Empire?'

The incredulity was evident in the desperate timbre of Edgar's voice, forcing a brief smile to appear on Stephen's lips. Head bowed, he sighed heavily and said, 'Along with his other cousin Czar Nicholas!'

'Indeed! Unless they think our ultimatum is *just* a bluff.' Edgar shook his head, and pocketing his brother's letter he drained his glass.

'How do you intend responding to Charles's concerns?'

'I think it's mostly bluster. As far as I am aware Daniel has given me no reason to think he may seek my permission to ask for Olivia's hand, nor do I believe she would readily accept him. I can see there is a bond between them, but whether it goes beyond a mutual interest in literature, I am inclined to doubt.'

Edgar checked his watch and rose from his seat; Stephen rising also, accepted his uncle's hand. He didn't feel as relaxed about the strength of Daniel and Olivia's friendship as Edgar did, however, the sombre mood which had descended over the evening was tangible as the deadline hour of the Government's ultimatum to Germany approached. Their family issues trivial compared to the stark reality facing the country by the day's end.

Covington, Devonshire – August 5th

Alex woke that morning to absorb the stark reality the country was going to war. The print room at the *Covington Echo* the previous day had been buzzing with speculation that Britain would be dragged into conflict, along with a feverish atmosphere, the likes of which Alex hadn't seen since news broke that *RMS Titanic* had sunk on its maiden voyage. The paper's editorial would be supportive of the Government's position and the banner headline for Friday's edition would be stark. He couldn't wait to see Laura's reaction to the news, which he expected to be fearful. She would, he thought, urge him in the most robust terms not to volunteer as she was instinctively cautious, and he thought that on this he might welcome her caution, although heeding her advice would put him at odds with many of his print room colleagues on the *Echo* as several apprentices had stated their intention to enlist, until the gaffer brought war talk to an abrupt end.

For himself, Alex couldn't claim the same confidence as his colleagues, and was acutely aware of the impact this conflict could have on their lives. The plans for their future, which with a gentle smile she invariably preferred to call *his* plans. How would she feel if conscription was introduced, leaving him no choice but to heed the call to arms?

He wasn't entirely sure why Britain had got itself involved with a conflict which had been threatened for weeks. He had kept his own counsel while the conversation about volunteering had been rife, but he was certain it was a subject to which the print room would return whenever the gaffer's back was turned. He knew he was no coward, but couldn't help wondering if some of their bravado was for effect.

He was, however, certain of one thing: however subconscious it may previously have been, the gentle pace with which his life had progressed thus far had shifted irrevocably. An act of violence committed by an idealistic adolescent of a similar age, in a city at the opposite end of Europe, had altered the course of history, and whatever direction the ensuing conflict may pull him from this tiny backwater of Devon, as in many such communities across Britain, nothing would ever be the same again.

Daniel looked at Stephen warily. His friend having finally responded to one of his many requests to meet, and although he understood his friend's prevarication in recent weeks, it had been a delay he was not accustomed to. His most recent telegram had been delivered last night to which Stephen had replied this morning. He could see his expression was pale, and he couldn't help wondering how Daniel might cope with the realities of conflict, when his regiment was called.

'So it's war!' he said sombrely, and Stephen smiled, the timbre of his voice so typically Daniel, who had never been inclined to reflect intently on matters of state. That he had little knowledge of what his job at the Foreign Office involved, although he routinely inquired out of politeness.

In many respects Daniel's life was held in abeyance, shaped by a destiny that would only be realised once his father, the current Earl Royston, died. Stephen had confidence that once confronted with that reality, his friend would rise to the challenges involved in running the estate, but he suspected Daniel was woefully ill-equipped emotionally to confront the harsh reality of war, and the potential dangers it could spell for the way of life that he had been raised to anticipate from birth. That reality did, however, bring one very pressing matter into sharp focus, but he had no more courage with which to voice it than he suspected his friend had.

He knew from having stood in the grand hall at *Javrons* that many generations of Swiffen men had fought for their country and paid a price for their valour. As the only son he couldn't foresee the Earl allowing Daniel to volunteer without first siring an heir. That would mean a swift marriage and the issue that he and Edgar had been discussing last night would be brought once more to immediate attention. It seemed so trivial to be discussing the issue now, as Stephen knew this afternoon the Prime Minister would make a formal announcement of the declaration of war with Germany to Parliament. For Daniel, it could not be overlooked and Stephen saw in his friend's expression that the prospect of him being forced to interrupt the direct line of ascendancy which had existed for generations of Swiffen men was *unpalatable*, but that it paled in comparison to the reality of combat.

Daniel took a deep breath as a footman in morning livery brought the coffee he had ordered into the study, overlooking the formal gardens in Cavendish Square.

'Did you really think it would come to this?'

Stephen smiled, 'To begin with no. It seemed too incredible, but as the month progressed it has become clear Austria were determined to have their demands for retribution met.'

'It seems staggering, given all we have learnt since, that at the very moment Olivia and I were strolling across Ashburn Park, a Serbian terrorist was seeking to shape the course of history.'

Stephen smiled, sipping his coffee, he couldn't recall his friend ever sounding so reflective. Daniel didn't usually do introspection. He had been known to thrive on his reputation as the life and soul of the party. Whatever impact the war was going to have on him, it would surely serve to inspire some marvellous poetry when his friend was motivated to put his thoughts on paper. Although right now the only emotion he could detect in Daniel was fear.

Setting his coffee aside, Stephen approached his friend. There were beads of sweat on his brow. Stephen knew he hadn't given his own thoughts about the reality of war much attention thus far, and guessed it might have been because he felt too close to it all. He knew that the Foreign Secretary, Lord Grey, didn't share the joyous outpouring of optimism some people were giving voice to, which bordered on hyperbole. He took his friend's head in both his hands, bringing it onto his shoulder. There was apprehension in Daniel's trembling voice, his complexion was almost grey. Stephen's memory took him back suddenly to when Daniel was first confronted by his tormentors at Eton. He had vowed then to defend his friend whenever he needed it, and by offering that assurance he was able to instil a semblance of confidence inside him. The battle front, if Daniel was destined to experience it, would be a vastly different arena on which to confront his demons than the fields of Eton, and this time Stephen couldn't tell Daniel Swiffen that it *was* going to be all right.

3

As the weeks rolled by, August slid gently into September, the harvest was gathered and life seemed to carry on as it always had, but there were signs of adjustment, some so subtle they were barely noticed, while others were the manifest evidence of a nation coming to terms with the reality of war.

Stephen Trentham was forced by pressures of work to shorten his trip to the Isle of Wight, but when the annual Cowes Regatta was cancelled due to the outbreak of hostilities, he abandoned his plans, accepting instead an invitation from Daniel, who was to accompany him on holiday, to an extended weekend at *Javrons*, albeit with the caveat that the Earl and Countess Royston would be in attendance as their annual month-long sojourn to the French Riviera had also been sacrificed.

Another reality that Stephen had quickly become accustomed to were the overcrowded platforms at major railway termini. Even the smaller stations gave way to an abundance of khaki-clad young men, volunteering for the Front in a spirit of bravado, although some were swiftly regretting their moment of impetuosity when the reality of bidding farewell to fussing mothers trying last-minute appeals to dissuade them, or having to witness the tears of heartbroken girlfriends, distraught that they too had failed to discourage them.

Stephen witnessed one such scene of familial heartbreak on a trip to Ashburn Park – his first since that fateful Sunday in June when personal matters had dominated his thoughts. Watching the scene unfolding before him he couldn't help thinking how trivial those concerns appeared now. He was going to Dorset at the behest of Edgar, as Uncle Charles had made no effort since to heal the rift which had opened up during lunch, largely due to Matthew's oafish behaviour. However, typically Charles had no hesitation about summoning the family when it suited him, and when they realised that Charles's main *gripe* was the increasing burden of responsibility for running Ashburn when so many of his estate employees were volunteering for action, Edgar had been incandescent at the crass insensitivity of Charles's attitude, while Stephen had been left aghast. He smiled now on recollection amid the din of chattering women bidding farewell to their men, making them promise they would try to keep themselves safe, with a forced sense of joviality masking the real fear that they might never see them alive again.

For his part Daniel, who had dined with Stephen prior to his Dorset trip, was still pondering his future, weighing up the limited options and waiting with dread the call-up from the regiment that generations of Swiffen men had loyally served. The outbreak of war had prompted the Earl to remind Daniel of his obligations to the estate, *stressing* the urgency to find a suitable wife who could provide him with an heir before – Daniel had smiled at this point, reciting his father's vernacular – *"he got his bloody head shot off."*

His mother tried to appear sympathetic, but while Elizabeth Swiffen made it clear that she didn't want her son to fight, she tried to present a united front standing solidly behind her husband as she generally did on such occasions, and this, Daniel had informed Stephen, was no exception.

He was looking forward to Stephen's arrival as it had been

a while since he had last entertained at the estate. He had considered extending the invitation to Andrew Restarick, which he knew would have delighted his younger sister Arabella, who had expressed some interest in him, however, he had decided against it, as Stephen and Andrew Restarick had never got on particularly well at Eton, and he wanted to gauge his friend's thoughts about approaching his uncle, Edgar Trentham, and seeking his permission to ask for Olivia's hand in marriage. It was a bold step, some might have said reckless, but Daniel's mind was set, and he wanted to broach the subject on home ground; his beloved *Javrons,* and *his* responsibilities to which had been drummed into him from earliest memory.

He couldn't be sure that Olivia Trentham would accept his proposal. She had very definite views about what she wanted from life and had never been shy about expressing them to him. Edgar Trentham had always encouraged her independent streak, and she had confided that sometimes he also feared it. For his part he had understood and acceded to Stephen's concerns about letting his feelings for Olivia spiral out of control. The outbreak of war, however, had changed everything and time was a luxury he could no longer claim.

Stephen arrived by taxi three days after his weekend at Ashburn Park which had, he confessed to Daniel, been as intense an ordeal as he had anticipated. Daniel also felt tense as he shook Stephen's hand on the gravel driveway. His smile was as thin as it was brief, and Stephen wondered at the source of his friend's anxiety, although it didn't take long for his suspicions to be confirmed that it was the high expectations that the Earl demanded of his heir, which Daniel had struggled to meet all his life, that had his friend feeling *so* ill at ease.

'Come let's get some air.' Daniel led Stephen away, having given instructions to a footman to take Stephen's bags to the guest room he always occupied on his visits to Javrons. They walked away from the house, with its Palladian façade across lawns still moist from the morning dew, and the slight chill in the air signalled that summer had taken its last bow, while autumn waited in abeyance, and the war which had been thrust upon them in a state of shock – as few could ever have guessed that it would come to this – was casting ever longer shadows, drawing people further into its sphere of influence from all echelons of society.

How long would it be, Stephen wondered, before all men of a certain age would be expected to heed the call to arms? The optimism with which the outbreak of war had been greeted – which he found misguided – had not abated with the passing weeks. The common view remained that victory was assured, the war would be short, and those who had volunteered would be home before Christmas.

'Look at them Stephen, *our* people. Labourers, gardeners, tenant farmers, the young footman who took your bag. Each of an age when they could be called to fight. How long before we're bidding them farewell as they leave perhaps for the last time? Or struggling to find words of condolence when news comes that they have been killed or are listed as missing in action. Haven't you asked yourself what the hell we're fighting for?'

Stephen shrugged, he looked solemn, and when he spoke it was in a flat monochrome tone. 'For King and country. For the Empire. The legitimacy of Belgian neutrality.'

Daniel grunted. 'That's still the official line? Take care my friend, you might start sounding like a politician'

Shaking his head, Stephen laughed. 'No Edgar is the only politician in the family. I'm just a humble civil servant.'

Stubbing his cigarette butt into the ground, Daniel touched the hollowed-out bark of a birch tree into which as a child he had carved his name alongside that of a girl whose father had worked on the estate. Smiling, he recalled the memory. 'I must have been about seven or eight years old when I carved that

22

declaration of my total devotion. It was childish nonsense as nothing could have come of it naturally. Imagine my parents reaction? Then of course it was purely instinctive.'

'Did you seal this liaison with a kiss?'

'Several I imagine. I think the initial attraction was that she was totally unlike my sisters, but I was aware even then that marriage for men like me isn't about instant attraction, or unbridled passion. It's *all* about duty. The Old Man's favourite word which he has been drumming into me ever since war was declared. He is convinced I will be killed you know. *"That I am ill equipped to cope with the reality of action,"* is another of his favourite lines and the prospect of having to fight terrifies me, but he cannot countenance my call-up until I've sired a legitimate heir, and that means marriage as soon as possible.'

'I'm guessing he hasn't offered any names as viable candidates?'

Daniel blanched, horrified by the prospect. 'No. Heaven forbid! That would be *intolerable*. Although the responsibility would be delegated to my mother and I don't find that any more palatable. Perhaps they see me as a lost cause in respect of the marriage market, which of course isn't an option.'

For a moment Stephen pondered the possibility that the Earl and Countess Royston knew about Daniel's *proclivities*, and for the sake of expediency had chosen to ignore them, but shaking his head he dismissed the idea, as Daniel would have confided that earth-shattering news to him. He acknowledged that gossip was rife in certain circles and several of Daniel's Eton adversaries never showed any inclination to be discreet, and despite his best efforts to protect, Stephen knew his friend hadn't always *erred* on the side of caution.

'Have any of your sisters' friends ever been put forward?' Daniel shook his head. 'Emily has grown apart from me somewhat and as for Arabella, she's more interested in cultivating an interest from Andrew Restarick to assist me.'

Stephen's expression darkened as he failed dismally to conceal his sense of shock and disapproval. His tone scathing, he said, 'Seriously? Is Andrew Restarick the man she's pinning her hopes on?'

'She is infatuated, although I'm not sure to what extent. Massaging his fragile ego has become a pet project of hers and whatever I might say to discourage her falls upon deaf ears. I believe she may actually find *"The Little Boy lost"* demeanour strangely attractive, and she has convinced herself she's going to save *him.*'

Daniel shook his head at this and the look of disdain on his face told Stephen his friend was as sceptical of this claim as he was. 'Besides Stephen, I know that although you and Andrew never took to each other, he has always been loyal in his friendship with me, and as you will recall, I wasn't especially overwhelmed with such friends back then.'

Stephen nodded grimly, accepting that the extent of Andrew Restarick's reliability as a friend was never likely to be a subject that he and Daniel would agree on. He retrieved a gold cigarette case from his jacket pocket and snapping it open, offered it to Daniel, which he declined. They continued sauntering in a companionable silence and then Daniel said, 'I thought we might take a ride after lunch if you're interested.' Stephen nodded gently and Daniel smiled. Feeling his spirits rise, he kept his thoughts to himself, convinced it presented him with the ideal opportunity to state his case for approaching Edgar Trentham on the delicate matter in hand.

★ ★ ★

Sunlight dappled the trees at the perimeter of the de Valois mansion in the 16th arrondissement. Paris looked splendid in its late afternoon hue with late summer gently giving way to autumn. Etienne de Valois liked the view from his master

24

bedroom, and half turning he smiled, thinking how much he admired the view within as well.

Eloise Chagal, his mistress, lay in bed, her head propped against her hand, rich brunette curls spilling onto the pillows. A mischievous smile curved the corner of her perfect bow-shaped mouth. A very kissable mouth, Etienne thought, with amusement lighting his eyes. She had the look of a woman who knew she had given intense sexual pleasure to her man and that she was as satisfied with her efforts in the bedroom as *she* knew he was. It tore at his heart knowing that, given what he was about to do, however much he *knew* it had to be done.

He referred to her as his mistress invariably with a glint in his amber-flecked eyes. Although strictly speaking she wasn't as he was as yet unmarried. He could have contemplated having Eloise as his wife, knowing that in the bedroom she could satisfy his every need, but in the mansions of the 16th arrondissement and the chateaux of the Loire Valley, she would never be accepted, and for this reason he would have to sacrifice her. To let her go and do it as swiftly and as painlessly as possible. He turned back to her as she gave him that *come hither* look and immediately he felt his resolve weakening. He liked to project himself as the charismatic confident man, but if truth be told he was in thrall to Eloise Chagal and beholden to his mother, Solange de Valois, whose dictum he was going to obey and by executing *her* demand he knew he would be breaking Eloise's heart.

He approached the four-poster bed with its maroon and gold covering, which matched the silk drapes at the window, both of them carrying the intricately woven crest of the de Valois family. Pulling him closer, she ran her index finger down his perfectly muscled abdomen to the waistband of his trousers, and the exquisite softness of her touch provoked the first thrust of his arousal. He leaned onto the mattress which took his weight as Eloise began combing her fingers through his sable coloured hair, which shone blond in the dappled autumnal light of late afternoon. She could sense he was ill at ease, his demeanour was that of a hesitant, troubled man.

'What?' she asked, letting the silken sheet fall to reveal one creamy white breast, and Etienne breathed deeply, his arousal hardening as he fought against the urge to take her again for one last time. How cruel would that be? Knowing as he did what would follow, although he had never promised her anything and he had always believed that she understood. They were lovers. That was all they were ever to be, but losing her, having to let her go, wrenched at his heart, although in truth he shouldn't let it. He had allowed himself to feel too strongly at least that was what his mother had told him on his most recent visit to the chateau the previous weekend, when Solange de Valois issued her ultimatum, with every expectation that it would be obeyed.

He kissed Eloise passionately on the mouth as they sank into each other's arms onto the bed. He planned to lose himself inside her once more, to arouse her to orgasm with each powerful thrust, and at the moment they climaxed together he wanted to have found the courage to reach the most gut-wrenching decision of his life.

An hour later Etienne sat in a chair nursing a Cognac. He was dressed again although his white evening shirt remained unbuttoned. Eloise, utterly sated by the latest session of lovemaking was still asleep. He had rung for two glasses to be sent up, although she didn't normally indulge, he anticipated she might be grateful for one this evening after he had told it was over; that he couldn't see her again and that she must not call again at the Mansion de Valois because he will have instructed his staff that she should not be permitted entry. It was brutal and he acknowledged that it made him look arrogant and callous, but he was limited in his options. While he detested himself for it, he had no choice. His mother held all the cards, and she had indulged his dalliance for as long as it suited her, but now she had played her hand her way and that was that.

Eloise woke to find the space beside her in the giant bed empty. She ran her palm across the sheet he had vacated and felt that it still held his warmth. She breathed in the intoxicating aroma of his scent and, looking up, she saw him, his face a brooding mask in the diminishing evening light.

'Why aren't you in here? Beside me.'

'Because it is over Eloise. We must not continue seeing each other. When you leave this evening it will be for the last time. You must not come here again!'

Eloise shook her head. Rising she let the sheet fall and seeing her naked splendour again he turned his head, willing himself to remain *unmoved*.

'No! I don't accept that!. I *won't!*'

'Oui. You must!'

'This is her doing. Your mother! The Corsican witch!'

'Enough! You must not speak of her in those terms.'

'Why not? I know that you despise her for the control she exercises over you. The ways in which she seeks to manipulate you to her will.'

'She has only the best interests of the de Valois family in mind. Its reputation and status in French society guides her decisions.'

'She plays you like the puppet and you dance to her tune!' Angry now her eyes blazing, she spat the words at him, with a vehemence he had never have imagined her capable of. Eloise was kneeling at the edge of the bed now, and Etienne standing with his fists clenched at his side took several deep breaths to compose himself. He had never seen her so hurt as she was now by his rejection, but her pride would not permit her to let him see her tears.

'I have dreaded telling you this as it's the hardest thing I've ever had to do, but your manner has made it easier because you have behaved exactly as my mother predicted you would. As – and these *are* her words not mine – exactly as a peasant girl from Rouen might!'

Eloise reached up to strike him, but Etienne anticipating her action parried the blows and captured both her wrists in his hands.

'Pity you're not so discerning about taking a peasant girl to your bed.'

Etienne smiled. 'In my bedroom the void in our social class is not so obvious, in other areas however, it is more like a chasm.'

Eloise wanted to spit her words at him, but she knew it would only confirm his mother's low opinion of her, for the words that he had thrown at her were the ones Solange de Valois would have used, and her weak, pathetic vessel of a son was merely the messenger.

'Lâche!' she screamed at him as she climbed from his bed, but Etienne was already at the door. Struggling for composure now as his pride had been wounded, he said quietly, 'I will leave you to dress and then I will see you in my salon.'

'Why Etienne? Is that where you plan to pay me off like a whore?!' Etienne shook his head. He didn't blame her for feeling *so* angry but he refused to be labelled thus. Marriage to Eloise wasn't something he had ever contemplated any less than he had with anyone. His mother had been more than patient in waiting for him to marry, but every girl she had ever presented had failed to elicit even a flutter of interest from him, never mind ignite a spark. A murmured acknowledgement that the latest candidate was mildly passable was invariably all he had to offer, but the outbreak of war had changed everything for Solange, and the time for indulgence had reached its conclusion.

He took his leave, descending the stairs wearily, he strolled into the salon and waited. He had no intention of paying her off, as he had never looked upon her as a whore or ever treated her as such, so the accusation was unworthy of her.

He had, however, purchased a small gift for her which was locked in the wall safe, but he was hesitant about giving that to her now. Eloise descended the stairs with a *hauteur* she didn't feel, but she was determined not to display any more of the hurt she felt because she still loved him, and because she believed he would regret the decision he had made this evening. By then it would be too late because he was weak. He didn't make the important decisions in his life and he lacked the courage to go against his mother's will. He hid behind tradition and the status of the de Valois name, but she doubted that gave him much solace and she *knew* that he would miss the carnal pleasures she had given him. He had placed the gift he had bought in a black velvet bag, which he removed from the safe when he heard her footsteps on the stairs.

'I want you to have this, *please*…'

Eloise eyed the bag suspiciously, unable to resist one parting barb. 'Severance pay for your mistress? How gallant you can be with gestures which mean nothing.'

He pushed his hand forward and nodded, urging her to take the bag. His manservant had opened the front door, and Eloise left. Immediately the chill autumn air hit her as she stood on the threshold and half-turned, but Etienne couldn't force himself to say goodbye because they both knew he didn't want to. The maroon and gold crested drapes moved slightly telling Eloise that he was watching her departure from his life and she half-smiled, hoping it was killing him to see her go. As she turned onto the curving boulevard which was lined with many such mansions as grand as his, she pulled back her shoulders and continued walking away It was only when she came to the end that she felt the salty sting in her eyes, that she realised she had succumbed to tears.

★ ★ ★

The Javrons Estate – Hertfordshire

Lunch had been a tense affair during which Stephen had been quizzed by the Earl for his views on how the conflict might develop, and how long he thought it would last. Arabella, the youngest of Daniel's two sisters, tried valiantly to divert the conversation away from the war, but she was treated to ignorance from the Earl and disapproving looks from the Countess. While Daniel, fearing he was the source of his father's *ire*, fidgeted uncomfortably throughout, wishing the meal would end.

Daniel and Stephen had their mounts saddled, having made their excuses to leave as swiftly they could manage, and were now gently trotting away from the house, with its curving drive and the magnificent Palladian façade. Daniel half-turning in his saddle, looked back at the house.

'Magnificent isn't it? I could never fall out of love with this estate. Our friends at Eton and Oxford who boasted endlessly about how they enjoyed their country weekends at one estate or another often ignored *Javrons*, probably to goad me, but it has its virtues and its sense of tradition, the same as Blenheim or Chatsworth.'

Stephen smiled, thinking how Edgar might react to what Daniel was saying. Given how much trouble the Lords had caused the Asquith Government, he doubted his uncle would ever be so nostalgic talking about an estate like *Javrons* or the others Daniel had mentioned. He had decided during lunch that he would confront Daniel's diffidence and cut through to the root of his concerns.

'What is it Daniel? I know my invitation came with strings attached.'

'It's Edgar. I wanted to sound you out, prior to approaching him – although I'll admit the prospect terrifies me – to seek his permission to formally propose to Olivia. I think our friendship has…'

'You're not serious?' Stephen's dark look matched his mood.

'Of course. You've just sat through lunch with the Old Man – sorry the Earl. His patience with me is wafer thin. I *must* act quickly and find a wife.'

'So my cousin, who I'm guessing you will promise to love and honour, meets your needs, although we both know you'll do neither and you're asking for what Daniel? My assistance, my approval? Maybe even my blessing?'

'No Stephen, your guidance about how best to approach Edgar. I guess what I am really hoping for is reassurance that he will hear me out, give my intentions towards Olivia the respect they deserve.'

'How can he Daniel, when they clearly don't!' Stephen dismounted at this point, turning his back on Daniel and trying to marshal his anger.

'It's not that Olivia would be getting nothing in return. Were she to accept my proposal, she would become the Viscountess Swiffen.' He expanded his hands smiling, 'With all that entails…'

Stephen was seething with anger. 'Does that include the likelihood that she could be a widow within months, before she has even reached the age of maturity. A husband who can never love her in the manner she deserves to be loved?'

Stephen whacked his riding crop against the trunk of a tree so hard it made Daniel wince, then he turned on his friend. 'You've deceived me Swiffen. You assured me that weekend at Ashburn that you understood my concerns regarding my cousin, and yet now you expect me to what? Acquiesce – I daresay even encourage her to embark upon this folly? This is *unforgivable!*'

'I'm sorry that you feel this way, but I am determined to seek Edgar's permission and ultimately it will be Olivia's decision.'

31

'You will destroy her chances of a happy marriage if you proceed with this plan. You have already said more than once, that you feel ill-equipped emotionally to face the reality of military action. So if she were to accept she could be moving from wedding white to mourning in a matter of months, if not weeks, and if you should survive what lies ahead of her? An heir and a spare, and then her wifely duties will be done?! So *no* Daniel, not with my blessing!'

4

Alex sat with his arm around Laura's waist in the dappled sunlight of an autumnal evening. He felt increasingly pressured in the print room at the *Echo* as many of the younger staff were declaring their intention to volunteer on a daily basis. Laura gazed at him, aware of how troubled he was by the perception his peers had of him and of the expectations being placed upon him.

'They can't force you to volunteer against your wishes,' Laura urged. 'There's no nationwide conscription as yet, thankfully.'

'That maybe only a matter of time though. The *Echo's* owners are struggling to retain their staff, and some of the older retired typesetters are being urged to come back. If I were to become the youngest typesetter in the print room, it may look as if I'm reluctant to fight.'

Laura pulled Alex's arm tighter around her waist, thus demonstrating her instinct to bind him ever more closely to her. She couldn't help being sensitive to his predicament, even if it hadn't softened her opposition to seeing him volunteer. She sought her father's views on the issue, but George Weston had been typically pragmatic, however diplomatic in his response.

'You'll have to reconcile yourself to the possibility of him going eventually lass. I know it's hard on you, but I've never been convinced by all the optimism that it will be over soon. I can't see our boys returning victorious before Christmas as some of 'em in the public bar at the Plough. You've seen for yourself how crowded our platforms are with young men in their khaki uniforms, wondering what they've signed up for, and realising perhaps that volunteering isn't all that it's cracked up to be.'

Laura had stubbornly wiped away the stray tear from her green eyes. She had resisted her father's instinct to embrace her, as she wanted to appear strong, and lounging now in her lover's arms, she remained resolute in her determination to dissuade Alex from volunteering for as long as she could, and she stuck out her chin determinedly. Kissing him lingeringly on the mouth, they didn't see Stoughton's stealth-like approach, until they heard his lewd whistling.

'Still wasting your time on this boy when it's a man you need, Laura.'

Alex's instinct was to stand up and lay one on him, but Laura's hold on him was vice-like.

'A lecherous bully is the last thing I will ever want Stoughton, so just go away!'

'As you please,' Stoughton sneered derisorily as he strode away.

'He's vile!!' Laura said vehemently, as soon as the head porter was out of earshot.

'I don't know why your father has to put up with him, as he's *so* rude and useless.'

'Truth be told, Dad says he can't fault his work ethic when he puts his mind to it. His rude manner as you say is intolerable, but however much Dad complains, it falls on deaf ears. The regional manager at Exeter refuses to transfer him.'

'You don't think he might have an ally where it matters? Someone who is willing to cover his back.'

Laura made a moue with her mouth. 'It wouldn't surprise me, although I don't give Stoughton anymore thought than I really have to.'

Alex pulled Laura closer, urging her head down to cushion against his chest. He kissed the top of her head and they fell into a companionable silence, watching the orange orb of the sun dipping lower towards the horizon as the chilly breeze of a September evening caused them both to shiver.

The Swiffen House – Cavendish Square

Daniel was grateful that Edgar Trentham had agreed to meet him and had acceded to do so at Daniel's home. He suspected his friend might have indicated to his uncle the reason for this meeting as he had heard nothing from Stephen since he abruptly left *Javrons* two weeks earlier.

The manner of Stephen's departure had cut deep, as it was *so* unnecessary, as ultimately it would be up to Edgar to grant him permission to propose and Olivia's to accept him. If Edgar thought it was a business meeting relating to the publication of Daniel's first volume of poetry, he gave no indication other than to confirm that his partner would be taking day to day responsibility for the business due to the hostilities. Daniel did detect impatience in his demeanour. Edgar checked his watch for a third time and turning to a slightly nervous Daniel, he said, 'I don't wish to appear rude but I am due in the Commons for an important division. So could we get to the crux of the matter: Why you wanted to see me this evening.'

Daniel smiled wanly. He had never sought a father's permission to propose before, so he had no idea regarding protocol and he wouldn't be in a rush to consider it now were it not for the outbreak of war. He had been successful at holding his father's demand for a legitimate heir at arm's length for some years, but the war robbed him of the luxury of waiting, as he knew his regiment could call him any day now.

'It's Olivia!'

Edgar turned sharply. 'What about her?'

'I wish – I mean I seek your permission to ask for her hand in marriage.'

Edgar smiled indulgently. So Charles had been *right* damn him! His elder brother had intimated that this was where the Swiffen heir's–Charles's words interest was leading, and he was surprised that Stephen hadn't given him forewarning.

'I see. I take it you've never approached a father on this subject before?' Daniel shook his head. He could feel his palms were clammy with sweat. Where the hell was the coffee he had requested? The latest footman was a major disappointment. Although he wasn't alone in that. Domestic staff were leaving their employers in droves to heed the call to arms.

'I am very fond of Olivia. We have become very close. I would be honoured to have her as my wife!'

'I am relieved to hear it, and you would be extremely fortunate to have her as your wife. You don't claim to love her though. You say you're merely fond of her. Is that really the solid basis on which to ask for a lady's hand in marriage? For a lifetime commitment.'

Daniel smiled. He reached for the bell to summon the footman, but hesitating he looked Edgar squarely in the eye. 'Has Stephen forewarned you of my intention to seek your permission?'

Edgar shook his head slowly. Smiling he said, 'So Stephen was aware of what you had planned. Interesting that my nephew didn't mention it, or try to speak favourably on your behalf.'

'He wouldn't do that Sir, because he doesn't support me in my wishes regarding Olivia. I think we may have fallen out on the subject as he cut his visit to *Javrons* short, and we haven't spoken since.'

Edgar nodded his head slowly. 'I see. Although you still haven't answered my question. How can you expect to have my permission to ask Olivia if you cannot say that you love her, and be prepared to offer the lifetime commitment?'

'With respect Sir, men of my generation cannot guarantee that once we have been sent to fight that the next twenty-four hours won't be our last.'

Edgar tapped the top of a winged armchair and smiled, the first sign of exuberance that Daniel had seen in his guest.

'So we come to the crux of the issue. The war! The underlying motive behind your request. The reason you want my daughter to commit her future to you now is so you can sire an heir, thus continuing the unbroken line of hereditary ascendancy in your family!'

Daniel gulped an indrawn breath. He knew Edgar Trentham was an astute man, but he hadn't anticipated his motives being analysed so crudely.

'Yes. Should Olivia feel inclined to accept my proposal she would attain the honour of becoming the Viscountess Swiffen.'

Edgar suppressed a smirk. 'A status which, you'll forgive me, carries considerable more honour and a greater degree of significance in your eyes than it does mine and which, as you've already pointed out, comes with the real possibility of her being left a widow. So I am intrigued Daniel, why you think I would wish to inflict such a title on her, when it carries no more hope of a long and happy marriage than if she were being offered the prospect of becoming Mrs Smith?'

Daniel inclined his head slightly. 'No, put in those terms, I cannot see why it would be easier for her to accept, but were we madly in love as you say we should be, wouldn't that make the *burden* of widowhood all the more difficult? The country is at war Mr Trentham, as you know only too well, and many young men and women are going to have to confront the realities of grief.'

Edgar looked into Daniel's eyes. He didn't see a bad man, but a very confused one, whose view of the world and its priorities differed greatly from his own. A man who carried the burden of his responsibilities heavily and contemplated the horrific reality of war with a genuine sense of dread. He hadn't heeded Charles's concerns about the prospects of a match between Daniel and Olivia. He would have his doubts about whether Daniel was strong enough to take on his daughter. For the last two years he had been greatly concerned that he was going to lose her to the cause of women's suffrage, and he had feared that sphere of influence all the more because of his political allegiance. War and a swift marriage – a loveless marriage – wasn't something he would ever want for her either, so he knew without hesitation that he couldn't give Daniel his permission, just as he knew that as a gentleman Daniel Swiffen wouldn't approach Olivia without it. It was probably one of the hardest decisions he had ever made, but as a father he saw no viable alternative that would offer his beloved daughter any hope of a happy marriage. While for Daniel Swiffen, and many young men like him from every class, hope was all that they had.

'I am afraid the answer is no Daniel. I cannot grant you permission to ask for Olivia's hand. I'm sorry for that, but I ask you respectively that you don't ask me to reconsider, as I won't be changing my mind. I wish you luck in finding the right girl to become the next Viscountess Swiffen, just as I wish you will return safely from whatever horror this wretched war has in store for you.'

Edgar inclined his head and making for the door he checked his watch, grimacing, he thought he might still make it to the Commons and contribute to the debate, before the division bell sounded. 'I bid you goodnight Viscount Swiffen.'

'And you Edgar. I thank you for allowing me a hearing. I

won't pretend that I am not disappointed and had I persuaded Olivia to accept, I would have tried my best to make her happy.'

Edgar inclined his head and left, while Daniel distraught, slammed his fist down on the top of the winged armchair and summoned the footman again, determined to vent his fury.

In the weeks that followed Daniel reconciled himself to the finality of Edgar's decision, and began gradually to overcome his disappointment and to apply himself to the task of finding a suitable wife, with whom he could sire a legitimate heir. He had never sought a love match, so he had no expectations in that regard, although he had grown increasingly fond of Olivia Trentham and felt he could have been happy with her; when he viewed the issue objectively, he began to understand why Edgar had reservations and so he could respect them.

There had also been a subtle shift in emphasis when it came to his dealings with his publisher. Edgar's partner Cedric Westmacott had been training his son to take a greater interest in the business. Parliamentary demands meant Edgar was forced to take a diminished role, so Daniel's luncheon date to discuss the final promotional strategy for his volume of poetry had been delegated to the nervous Austin Westmacott, a very earnest – if somewhat awkward – young man, who Daniel discovered quickly had developed an enormous crush on Olivia that he was evidently embarrassed about, as it appeared she was barely aware of him among all the talented flamboyant writers she got to meet by having taken such a large interest in her father's business.

They were sat in a crowded restaurant in the heart of Bloomsbury which Austin had chosen, and Daniel was ordering his entrée when Olivia came storming up to their table, clearly angry, as a flustered Austin rose to his feet and began mumbling. Olivia only partially acknowledged him, which Daniel found slightly amusing, until he realised the purpose for gate crashing their luncheon was to turn her *ire* on him.

'Daniel Swiffen I am very disappointed in you. Extremely so in fact.'

Other patrons turned to look in their direction, as Austin Westmacott mewled desperately, which Daniel genuinely thought was a prelude to tears. Olivia looked at Austin, witheringly, and turning back to Daniel she said, 'I understand that my father has had to delegate his responsibilities elsewhere, but I cannot understand why I should be snubbed. We have enjoyed many such luncheon engagements since the company decided to publish your poetry, so I am at a loss to understand *why* you have neglected to invite me today. As I put a great value on our friendship, which is more than would appear you do.'

'Isn't she fantastic?' shrieked Austin, which earned him another look of withering disdain from Olivia, who turned back to Daniel, her brow raised questioningly.

'I don't believe this is either the time or place to have such a conversation. In fact I am bound by assurances I gave him at our meeting, so I think it is a conversation that you should be having with him. He can explain.'

'Explain what? What assurances?' Olivia's voice was still raised and the maître d' had already indicated an inclination to intervene on all his patrons' behalf but Daniel urged him to wait.

'I insist you ask your father to explain.'

'On the contrary Viscount Swiffen I think that *you* as a gentleman should explain your actions. Our friendship is our business, not my father's.' So if I have upset you in some way, or worse you have decided that I have out run my usefulness to you, then I believe I *merit* the courtesy of you telling me so, face to face.'

Daniel was appalled. How could she ever think she would no longer be of use to him, or that their friendship didn't matter? The reality couldn't have been further from the truth and in that moment he resented Edgar bitterly for bringing this situation to the fore. He wasn't going to be able to keep his promise now and Edgar only had himself to blame for whatever *hurt* Olivia felt from the truth that she was forcing *him* to reveal.

'Ok. I shall explain as you insist, but not here. At my house in Cavendish Square. Your father asked me not to seek you out, with what we discussed, but you *deserve* the truth.'

Daniel didn't envy Edgar having to explain the *rationale* for declining his request, as he was sure Olivia would demand it from her father after he had revealed his version of events. At this point Austin spoke, as if to remind them, that he was still there. 'Excuse me Viscount Swiffen, but we haven't concluded our business as yet.'

Olivia turned to him, 'Austin I'm afraid what Daniel and I have to discuss is a little more urgent than some details about the promotional strategy for his book. I am sure Cedric will understand and I shall explain to him if it would help.' Austin mumbled something they barely heard. For himself Daniel smiled admiringly at how Olivia Trentham, who wasn't a salaried employee of *Trentham & Westmacott*, could exert such authority, as it served as further evidence had he required it, of what a remarkable young woman she was.

They left Austin to settle the bill for the drinks they'd had, taking a taxi to Cavendish Square. Ushering Olivia into the same room in which he had received Edgar. Inviting her to sit down, which she declined, he offered her a cigarette, which she thought about accepting but demurred, keeping her gaze trained on him while he lit his with fumbling fingers.

'I sought your father's permission to ask for your hand in marriage.' Olivia took a long deep breath, into a silence which felt to Daniel, excruciatingly long. Finally she spoke, 'I see. What was his response to your request?'

'He declined to give it, and I got the distinct impression that he preferred you to be unaware that I had asked, although he did indicate that he thought it was best that I saw less of you, which is why I guess you were not made aware of my luncheon date today.'

Olivia sneered derisorily. 'I doubt I would have been informed anyway. Not if Austin Westmacott had his way.'

Daniel dragged heavily on his cigarette. Other than seeing that she was incandescent, he was struggling to gauge how she might react.

'So my father decided that poor little Olivia was to be kept in blissful ignorance of the fact a man should want her hand in marriage. A future Earl no less. So hardly an unattractive suitor. Does he think his own daughter unworthy of becoming a Countess?'

'I can see that you are shocked and upset by this development, which is the last thing I wanted.'

'Yet you acquiesced in his deceit of me?'

'I was tempted to go against his wishes and to continue seeing you regularly but I had no idea how you felt, how you would have reacted to my proposal.'

'You could have asked me yourself.'

Daniel shook his head. 'That goes against protocol. I have too much respect for your father for that and...'

'What?'

'I asked Stephen's advice prior to speaking to your father, given how long we have been friends, and he was against me proposing.'

'Would you have any idea why they were *so* against the idea?'

Daniel was certain of Stephen's motives but he had no intention of discussing what they had called his *proclivities* with Olivia, so he relied on her father's misgivings, mainly the impact of the war.

'I know at some point my regiment, of which I am a reservist, will call me to action. I believe that was a motivating factor in your father's decision to decline his permission.'

Olivia slumped into the chair she had previously declined, shaking her head vigorously. 'So it is deemed acceptable in my father's eyes, for the Government of which he is a member, to encourage young men, the fruit of the nation's youth, to volunteer for war? For their wives and sweethearts to be left grieving, their children fatherless, while they turn a blind eye to the mindless slaughter of the trenches while commissioning posters saying your country needs you, but so exalted is *he* that his own daughter should be spared such a fate?'

Daniel took another deep drag on his cigarette. Olivia was making him nervous. He had never had doubts about her passionate adherence to certain issues but he had never heard her speak thus. Despite having failed to honour his promise to Edgar, he couldn't help wondering what an independently-minded woman would have decided had she been allowed the opportunity, and so feeling no further obligation to be discreet he was determined to ask.

'So if your father had consented and I had proposed would you have accepted?'

Olivia looked at him sharply. She took a deep breath and a slight smile curved the corners of her mouth.

'I don't know Daniel. That is the honest answer. I don't believe I am in love with you. Although I do recognise your obligations to the estate. The Earldom. That is a primary consideration for you. There would have to be something...' she placed her palm against her heart, adding, '...in here for me to accept. More than the bond of friendship we have enjoyed – but for me this is the real crux of the matter, that my father having invested so much in my education and given me so many options that many women don't have – the objective of all that should have been to equip me to make the decision for myself!'

Olivia's voice wobbled for the first time at this point, as

Daniel moved towards her, but she raised her hand to hold him off. She didn't want his sympathy, that much was clear. She had said how much she had valued their friendship and he genuinely hoped that it could survive this, but while he had respected Edgar's wishes in declining him permission to propose, he had to accept they had handled it poorly. They had underestimated Olivia's capacity for thinking independently. Her *zeal*. Now they would have to contend with her fury. That he believed was a price they should be prepared to pay.

5

With the autumnal rains there came an air of despondency for those who believed the hyperbole that the war would be short, brisk and swathed in the elation that came with victory. The reality was becoming harder to take and yet young men were still volunteering with the same determination that the first wave had marched through streets filled with cheering crowds in the sultry sunshine of early August.

To Laura's mind, the optimism with which the volunteers still marched to war was baffling, but she remained as determined as ever in not encouraging Alex to follow them. She was unfazed when he pointed out in a matter-of-fact way that he was one of the last few staff still working at the *Covington Echo* under the age of thirty. Her father was becomingly increasingly concerned by what appeared to be her intractable attitude to accepting that Alex would eventually have to volunteer. Some of the earliest casualties were already making their way home, invalided out, their war already over, although in some cases they were lucky to be alive. The sight of ex-servicemen with legs amputated below the knee, balancing precariously on crutches as they sold matches on street corners, was becoming more familiar in towns and cities across the country. Their futures looked bleak and George Weston was struck by the irony that the same people who formed the cheering crowds coming out to wave their flags as they went off to France, now barely noticed them as the wounded men who had returned, raising a dismissive hand when called upon to buy their wares. So *he* understood why Laura didn't want Alex volunteering, and a part of him hoped that Alex could hold out, but as he suspected, the longed for early victory wouldn't materialise he feared eventually nationwide conscription might become inevitable, and he didn't want to contemplate his beloved Laura having to confront the reality of Alex having no choice but to enlist.

His head porter, the wretched Charlie Stoughton, wasn't helping matters either, rather typically as he had witnessed two confrontations where Stoughton had been goading Alex about not having volunteered, and determined to avoid a confrontation George had intervened, telling the sneering Stoughton to get back to work. For his own part he was still trying to rid himself of the scourge of Stoughton's malevolent influence, but his bosses at Great Western were not encouraging, pointing out that manpower was short and as station master George had the authority over his porter, and he should have the discretion to use it. He had returned from that meeting in Exeter in a sombre mood while Alex, feeling no better, had felt the heat of Laura's wrath at the dinner table when the issue of volunteering was raised.

'I've had enough! All that people talk about is this wretched war! Which most of 'em felt would be over by now, that our men, and some of 'em just boys, were sure to be coming home in time for Christmas. Is it likely now? We've all seen them that have come home wounded, some looking bewildered. I saw a man alighting a train the other day with a empty sleeve pinned to his chest were his arm used to be, trying desperately to calm his mother, to stop her wailing in public. Where was the cheering crowd to welcome 'em home? That's the reality they don't want to see. Is that what you want to go off for? Just to avert a little criticism in the print room, which you used to call harmless banter.'

'Shh. Calm yourself lass,' George urged her.

'I will not calm myself! I love you Alex Conyer, and if you don't mind I want to go on loving you. Not mourning a memory! Oh what's the bloody point?' Laura, with a large serving spoon in hand, was poised to dish mashed potato onto three plates, instead she replaced the saucepan on the range with a clatter and holding her tears at bay, she now looked at her father and at the young man she hoped would one day become her husband, and shaking her head she realised she could hold her tears no more and she fled the kitchen, taking the stairs two at a time, until they heard her slam the bedroom door.

'She'll be all right lad.'

'Will she? I've never seen Laura so mad! I get it that she's scared. I'm scared. I suspect half the men who have volunteered already were scared, even if they daren't admit it. I don't want to be the last man in Covington under thirty who is pointed at in the street as the one who won't go to fight. I won't be that man George. I won't!'

George rose from his chair, shaking his head. He reached for his pipe from the mantelpiece above the fire, squeezing Alex's shoulder in a gesture of solidarity and encouragement.

'I know son. I'll speak to her. Try to get her to see the situation through your eyes. The accusation of cowardice can be a foul slur to hurl at a man and I wouldn't wish it on anyone. All the optimism with which people greeted the outbreak of war has turned to resentment, which is a dangerous emotion when it's foisted on others. Volunteering is becoming an expectation rather than a freedom of choice, and still there's no compulsion from the Government to do so.'

George lit his pipe, reflecting on the evening's events. They couldn't hear sobbing from upstairs so they guessed any tears Laura was shedding were silent ones. He glanced at the clock and then at Alex. They both knew they wouldn't be seeing Laura again tonight.

'So what *do* I do?' Alex heard the pleading tone in his voice. It wasn't the first time he had sought George Weston's advice and he suspected it wouldn't be the last. Aside from his maternal grandfather there was no other man he knew who had ever commanded his respect.

'Hold tight if you can. Tell whoever asks that you will volunteer when it is right for *you!* Not on their terms. Yours!'

The tension between Alex and Laura continued for a number of days as she saw no reason to lull him into a false sense that all was fine after her outburst, or that he could wear down her resolve. She didn't want him to rush into volunteering for a war that could still end as swiftly as many had predicted, although the prospects of that were becoming bleak. Laura was to witness for herself some of the criticism that Alex had been subjected to when they came back into Covington Station as a battalion of volunteers marched through the town, with an accompanying band, drums, cymbals et al.

They stopped briefly to view the scene and soak up the atmosphere when a plump middle-aged woman leaned into Alex and ominously whispered into his ear. 'You should be there, marching with them! So why aren't you? You look fit enough, so why haven't you volunteered?'

Alex was inclined to ignore her, although he had been shocked by the bluntness of a stranger, the content of her words being no different to what he had already heard, but Laura was having none of it. 'How dare you! Who the hell are you to goad him into volunteering? Doing Kitchener's bidding for him now are you? On his payroll!?'

When the woman, ignoring what Laura had said, reached into the pocket of her tight-fitting threadbare coat to retrieve a white feather she wanted to hand to Alex, Laura slapped it down, taking the feather she threw it aside, pushing at the woman in the jostling crowd. 'You vile interfering old witch!'

'I know it's hard on you luv but you've got to let him go. There's many a lass who's had to see her beau go off to fight. So what makes you any different?'

Laura lunged at her and would have readily tore the harridan's hair out, had Alex not stopped her. 'Don't you patronise me. You don't know us or anything about us. You just see a young man of fighting age and *assume* he's fit enough to fight.'

'He looks fit enough to me, but perhaps that's what is gnawing at you. You don't want him to go 'cos you'll miss him keeping you warm in bed each night.'

This brought roars of laughter from onlookers and Laura, clearly embarrassed, lunged at her again. 'You foul mouthed old hag! I would be surprised if you could remember the last time a man touched you!'

The woman blanched a deep shade of crimson as Laura struggled out of Alex's hold.

'A vicious tongue you've got there lass. You should be careful, it could get you into trouble.' The woman walked away treading her big feet on the white feather which had been trampled into the ground.

Alex looked at Laura, his eyebrows raised. 'Was that show for my benefit Laura, or your own?'

'She was the one handing out feathers. Do you want the likes of her branding you a coward? How dare she?'

'I chose to ignore her. As I choose to ignore all the snide remarks I've heard behind my back every day for the last month in the *Echo* print room. Those men know me and still they wonder why I haven't volunteered. Am I a conscientious objector, or just a coward? I don't want to go to fight in France! If I had seen it all as a big adventure I would have volunteered in August with the others, who couldn't wait. I've heard it's hell in those trenches, but what you will have to confront is the likelihood that one day, perhaps sooner than I want, I will have to go, and if you still chafe against me going then many more people will be questioning me, and we will have a lot more to contend with than that old witch.'

Laura bit on her bottom lip and Alex feared that tears were imminent, but he didn't rush to console her because Laura needed to hear it, as unpalatable as it was. Many young lives had perished on the battlefields of France and while he wasn't rushing headlong into the conflict as many of his peers, imbued with hyperbole had, he knew it was an inevitable consequence for a young man and to be seen not to have done his duty drew a shame far harsher; that fate he would not subject himself to, however hard Laura took his decision to go. He understood that the fear of losing him paralysed her, and he couldn't contemplate life without her, but she needed to reconcile herself to the reality of the world they were living in, and the sooner she faced that the better it would be for both their sakes.

Laura looked at him and as he smiled she wanted to embrace him, to hold onto him tightly, but he held back slightly. 'I need you to understand that I'm not planning to volunteer today or tomorrow or even the next because of what that wretched old witch said, but maybe soon, the price to pay for holding back will simply be too high. I don't want this to break us Laura, but the task is down to us both not to let that happen.'

Alex then took Laura into his arms hugging her close; they kissed briefly and in the dwindling autumnal light they walked the final paces into the station. Arm in arm, in companionable silence. Alex thought that perhaps the confrontation with the interfering old witch had been a blessing as much as a salutary lesson because he had protected Laura from much of the *wrath* he had been subjected to. It wasn't fair for him to lay all the blame on her as he had dug his heels in and hardened his reluctance to volunteer. He had never got the sense of optimism with which some many of his peers at the *Echo* had volunteered so readily, and Laura had been cocooned in her world which consisted of Covington Station and the station master's cottage.

She had witnessed the tearful platform farewells and the sombre homecomings from a distance, but Laura hadn't *felt* it until today. Alex hoped that she had changed her perspective of the war and what it meant for all of them.

6

Andrew Restarick was slighter and often maligned for looking considerably more effeminate than Daniel Swiffen – although these comments, first made when they were at Eton, were intended as insults issued by the likes of Crowley and Frobisher, so it was hardly surprising. Restarick had clung to Daniel like a limpet, seeming to draw strength from him, but Stephen Trentham was always concerned that Restarick's dependant nature was a drawback for Daniel, so an antagonism developed between Andrew and Stephen which continued on to Oxford and was never reconciled.

For his part Daniel liked Andrew from the time they met, and was inclined to indulge his dependency, and while he respected Stephen's concerns about not drawing attention to himself, thus making it easier for the likes of Crowley and Frobisher to seize any opportunity to bring him down, he knew he was never likely to earn their respect, so sacrificing Andrew's friendship to appease them was for him futile, and why he had never considered it. They met again quite by chance on Piccadilly, and Daniel insisted they have lunch the following day at his Club on Northumberland Avenue. Restarick, who usually gave such surroundings a wide berth, felt like a fish out of water, waiting nervously for Daniel to arrive. Giving the title Viscount Swiffen was bound to gain him access to the Club, even as a non-member, and although uncomfortable in what he had always considered overtly macho surroundings, his worst fears were confirmed when the oafish Frobisher, evidently over imbued with alcohol even in the middle of the day, approached him.

'Restarick! All a bit too red blooded for you this place, isn't it?'

Andrew could feel the clammy sweat on his palms and silently he willed Daniel to arrive. 'What do you want Frobisher?'

'Just being hospitable. There's no need to cry! Ha! Ha! You always were very prone to tears weren't you Restarick?'

'You were always very boorish, even without being in your cups, so some things never change.'

Frobisher made some condescending noise and, wobbling on his feet, nearly collided with a passing steward. Several older members gave him the evil eye, clearly disgusted with his behaviour, but he was oblivious to it.

'So who are you meeting? Which member of our Club have you got your eye on?'

Frobisher leaned so close into Andrew that he could see the deep blue of his irises, while Andrew was overwhelmed by the stench of stale alcohol on Frobisher's breath. 'Not that it's any of your business, I am having lunch with Daniel, Viscount Swiffen.'

Frobisher still rocking on his heels sniffed with derision. 'Still as close to Swiffen as ever are you? Shouldn't be surprised, you always were an exclusive duo. You let Trentham in when it suited, but you always wanted Swiffen all to yourself. Quite literally I believe. Although the word is out that Swiffen desperately needs a wife. He won't be allowed to do his bit for King and Country until he's sired an heir, and I've heard that Trentham's cousin is his intended. Is that why you've come to lunch? To re-establish contact in case your rival becomes family through marriage?'

Andrew was visibly uncomfortable now, as Frobisher was making a show of himself talking too loudly and Andrew fought the urge to blush. 'You're talking nonsense! I acknowledge there were difficulties between myself and Stephen at Eton, but that is resolved now. All in the past you might say.'

Frobisher, struggling to stand, leered at Andrew as two stewards arrived to take him away, just as Daniel arrived. Frobisher winked conspiratorially at Daniel as he was frogmarched away, and Daniel greeted Andrew, firstly with a handshake and then with an embrace.

'Sorry I'm delayed. Was Frobisher being a prig – sorry daft question. When is Frobisher not being a prig? Daniel led them to the leather-winged armchairs by the window and sitting down he lit a cigarette, offering his open case to Andrew, who took one, watching his friend's movements minutely.

The athletic grace of Daniel Swiffen was unmistakable and Andrew, although embarrassed by Frobisher's boorishness, had to admit that he *had* been infatuated with Daniel at Eton. An infatuation that Daniel had been flattered by and had even overtly encouraged.

'So how have things been?'

'Fine.'

'I wish I could say the same. I'm sorry, my mind is all over the place with the volume of poetry – my first being published – and the Old Man's constant urging me to find a suitable wife.'

Andrew smiled uneasily. He needed to know the truth about the Trentham girl. Could Daniel have found himself the wife that duty and his upbringing had always demanded he have? Although he hated to admit it, Frobisher had a point. If Daniel was betrothed to Olivia, it would inevitably bring him and Stephen closer together, while he would feel on the outside. One of the main reasons he had never reconciled his differences with Stephen Trentham was because he had never accepted the assertion that *his* indiscretions caused problems for

Daniel, which Stephen had endeavoured to minimise. It had hurt him deeply as Stephen was keen to place most of the blame on him when they had both been aware that one of Daniel's major faults was his tendency to be reckless. He had thrived on risk at Eton while Stephen tried to limit the damage and *his* inclination was to avoid it, but he acknowledged that with Daniel his resolve always weakened. He had never met a man like him.

Daniel smiled, drawing heavily on his cigarette. 'You should come to *Javrons* for the weekend. In fact I *insist* on it. I doubt my sister, Arabella, will ever forgive ——or even speak to me again should I fail to convince you. She has a bit of a crush I'm afraid. I fear she may be infatuated.'

Andrew blushed. Like Daniel he was expected to marry well but without the same imperative. He knew the Swiffens enjoyed an unbroken line of succession going back centuries, but that Daniel was unlucky in that for the first time in many years he was not just the only son, but that he had no male cousins of his generation.

He recalled now that they had spent many hours at Eton, playing chess in Daniel's rooms, and in the long winter months Daniel was inclined to sit in a hot bath while they played. Andrew freely had admitted sometimes to feeling hopelessly gauche in Daniel's company, because he always appeared so assured, and the first time Daniel had unselfconsciously stood up in the bathtub, asking Andrew to pass him a towel, the reaction it had provoked inside him had left Andrew crimson. Even thinking about it now caused his palms to sweat.

'Well?' Daniel leaned forward to stub out his cigarette, nodding encouragingly. 'Will you come?'

'Of course. Thanks for the invitation.'

Daniel laughed. 'I should probably let Arabella do the honours, even if it does breach formal protocol. I *confess* that I have little patience with such nonsense. What were you daydreaming about?' Daniel asked lightly, but Andrew took it as a criticism and bristled slightly. He had always tried not to let Daniel intimidate him, but readily accepted that he invariably fell short. He sought the other man's approval like it was a drug to which he was addicted, and the intervening years had changed nothing.

He could be jealous of Daniel and resent him accordingly, and yet he admired him at the same time. In some aspects the weekend at *Javrons* would be a kind of torture, but such were the extent of his contradictions he wouldn't have missed out on the weekend for anything.

'Good that is settled then.' Daniel summoned the waiter with a click of his fingers and ordered more drinks, while Andrew absorbed what his friend had said about his sister, Arabella, being infatuated with him. He couldn't be sure whether Daniel was speaking entirely in jest, but he doubted it would amount to anything more than a mild fascination at best on her part. Nor could he see any future for such a union. From what he knew and had been told about the Earl Royston, he couldn't imagine the *"Old Man"* – as Daniel always referred to his father, albeit affectionately – viewing him as a prospective husband and *thus* giving him consent to marry his youngest daughter.

'Perhaps you should consider asking your sister – Lavinia isn't it? – to join us for the weekend!'

Andrew tried to conceal his disappointment. 'Really?'

'Of course. Arabella will enjoy the company, and it will distract her having to play hostess. Ask her at least.'

'Of course,' Andrew said meekly, but he couldn't help hoping that Lavinia would politely decline the invitation because he selfishly wanted Daniel's company to himself.

Although she was genuinely surprised by the invitation, she received several days later, Lavinia Restarick accepted it readily, intrigued by what had prompted her brother's friend from

Eton to include her. She barely noticed Andrew's crestfallen response to her acceptance as he had pinned his hopes on her declining. He wasn't sure what her opinion of the Swiffen sisters was, although she had attended a few events at which she must have come into proximity with Emily and Arabella. He was going only for Daniel, albeit mindful of his friend's warning about his sister's interest, although he couldn't imagine how Arabella ever had the opportunity to develop an infatuation with him as they had only met previously on a few occasions, and not for some years. Was her interest in him genuine or was Daniel planning a ruse? It was hard to tell because so much conversation at social events centred around the war, as some of the news could be particularly grim and hard to hear when they heard that one or more of their circle had either been injured or killed in action. For this reason he understood why the Earl Royston was so concerned that Daniel secure the future of the title by marrying swiftly because once he was called to action his fate would be unknown.

They had barely discussed the war during lunch at his Club as Daniel had declared it a taboo subject. Andrew had his own concerns about volunteering for action, which up until now he hadn't felt compelled to reveal outside the circle of his family, but as a reservist in the Hertfordshire Regiment in which so many of the Swiffen men had served, Daniel's fate was more certain, and Andrew knew without having it confirmed, that the prospect of fighting scared the hell out of Daniel.

They sat now in the car that had been waiting for them at the station closest to the *Javrons* estate. Glancing at his sister, Andrew still couldn't understand what had motivated Daniel to extend the invitation to her, but he knew he could rely upon Lavinia for moral support.

'So how many times have you seen Daniel?'

Lavinia shook her head. Her grey eyes lively vivid. 'I can't be sure exactly, but not many. I recall him having spent some of the summer with us and then on subsequent occasions you were very disappointed when he had to decline. Can't you just let go of the intrigue that's eating away at you and accept it as an act of kindness, to both of us. I can't imagine why he would have an ulterior motive. Although I do understand that you wanted him to yourself.'

Andrew bristled angrily, pulling his hand away he turned sharply to look ahead of him. He usually found Lavinia's gentle teasing easy to handle but realised he was on edge today. 'What the hell is that barb meant to mean?'

'Exactly what I said. Come on Andrew, you have always been able to be *yourself* with me. You can trust me, *and* in my discretion. I knew you had a crush on Daniel Swiffen. I could see it the first time I met him. Besides I thought you said my inclusion this weekend was to distract his sister's attentions away from you.'

'It was. Although I'm yet to be convinced by his claim' Andrew stated flatly, embarrassed by his reaction.

Lavinia took his hand in her gloved one, squeezing it gently. 'Let's hope it does the trick then.' Andrew smiled weakly and swiftly turned his head to take in the view and to hide his predilection to blush away from Lavinia's forensic assessment.

Daniel greeted Andrew and Lavinia in the library, announcing that the Earl and Countess were spending the weekend with friends at another estate somewhere in Yorkshire. He was relieved because had his father been here, Lavinia would doubtless have been interrogated mercilessly and none too *subtly*. Daniel wanted to play the long game. In due course Arabella joined them in the library, offering her hand to Andrew which he bent to kiss, hesitantly and somewhat clumsily.

'We will leave you two ladies to get better acquainted, while we go for a stroll around the estate.'

'After we have had coffee Daniel. Why the hurry, unless you're upto something.'

'Absolutely not!' Andrew interjected a little too loudly, which earned him a sharp response from his sister, shocked by his vehemence, and a surprised one from Arabella, who curved a quizzical eyebrow at him, while Daniel, amused, slapped his friend good naturedly on the shoulder.

'No need to be *so* earnest. You're among friends and you'll learn soon enough not to react to Arabella's jesting. She has this instinct that leads her to believe that I'm usually upto no good.'

Arabella smiling, kneeled on the settee, her chin resting on her arm. 'That's usually because you are.'

Feeling foolish and ignoring Lavinia's look of censure, Andrew blushed slightly, fumbling in his pocket for a cigarette case, which once opened he offered round. Daniel took one and lighting it he drew heavily, the whirl of blue-grey smoke drifting upwards as he said, 'I think I should advise you that any topic of conversation is permitted this weekend, aside from the war.'

'And your marriage prospects,' Arabella added with a twinkle.

Daniel threw his sister a rueful glance and said, 'Ok the war and marriage are off the agenda until Monday and only to be tolerated then, if we've exhausted all others.'

Daniel gave Arabella a sharp cold look, but she remained unperturbed as he pulled the cord to summon the coffee be served. Sometimes Arabella pushed her luck, her jesting was too near the mark, and it made her appear insufferable. He had been genuine in his motives for extending the invitation to Lavinia, but Arabella seemed determined to undermine those motives with her challenging looks and barbed comments. He wasn't going to deny he would be assessing Lavinia as a potential bride, but as he couldn't guess what Andrew's reaction would be to him asking for Lavinia's hand, and *he* was still calculating the damage from his clumsy attempt to win Olivia's hand. He was sure his friend would be jealous as Andrew had once admired him slavishly, and although Daniel was flattered, it did nothing to change the situation. He needed a wife. Getting a moment alone to speak Lavinia Restarick would be quite a challenge, but Daniel knew he had to give it a try.

Meeting Andrew again by chance on Piccadilly had been fortuitous and it is said that fortune favoured the brave, so *now* was the time for him to be brave and bold. He saw it as an opportunity not to be wasted, but the damned formalities still got in the way in the polite society circles that his family moved in, *and* adherence to them had done him no favours when he formally approached Edgar Trentham. So he was inclined to slightly circumnavigate them this time by utilising his friendship with Andrew to – at the very least – gauge not only his friend's opinion, but also Lavinia's view of his prospects as a potential suitor. That his friendship with Andrew might suffer, similarly to how his friendship with Stephen had, was a risk that he was prepared to take, as he genuinely liked Lavinia, recalling how friendly and vivacious she had been the first time he had visited the Restarick home. He had been on those occasions, Andrew confided, cast in the role of the dashing knight as far as Lavinia had been concerned. So if that were to be his trump card again, he would have to use it wisely and know when to play it well.

Andrew Restarick was soaking in a bath, his head back; as he smoked a cheroot. When he heard a slight knock on the door, he hoped it might be Daniel who had, he felt, been slightly distant when they had gone for their stroll. Equally he feared it might be Arabella, and although that would be a brazen breach of protocol, he doubted Daniel's younger sister was ever a slavish follower of convention. He was relieved however, when the connecting door opened and Lavinia smiled.

'What do you want?' He knew his tone sounded petulant, but she would just have to live with it. Lavinia floated into the room, wearing a black silk night-gown and moved towards him, running a hand through the bubbles in the bathtub. 'Can a man not take a bath now without being disturbed by an irritating sibling?'

'I wondered how things were going? Have you managed to find out what Arabella's plans are for you?'

'No! I don't think she has any plan especially, and none that I would be interested in. I'm beginning to think that Daniel's insistence on including you in his invitation might have been a ruse. I can't see how Arabella would be interested in me when she would have her pick of suitors, being the daughter of an Earl.'

Lavinia nodded. 'Unless her pick has been killed, or badly wounded at the Front and she's been forced to re-evaluate her options. I mean she had other topics of conversation aside from you when we were alone. She has convinced herself that you need taking in hand which is nice I guess – albeit a little nauseating!'

Andrew ignored his sister's barb, his brow pleating. 'For what purpose?'

Lavinia shrugged. 'An unsuitable and unhappy marriage I guess.'

'You're not serious? This isn't a game Lavinia and I've told you she could have her pick of men.'

'Well she didn't use the M-word specifically, but that was the general drift of her conversation, and she was very keen to know if any debutantes had caught your eye and were seriously being considered as a future Mrs Andrew Restarick-unless and I'm sorry if this isn't what you want to hear, but maybe it's her brother, she trying to protect.'

Andrew looked sharply at her, trying to discern whether there was an iota of mirth in her voice, or the twinkle of a smile. Finding none. He groaned, 'From me you mean?' Standing up in the bathtub, strangely unconcerned about being naked in his sister's presence, he held out his hand for the towel. Lavinia bit her lip.

'Even the fact that you won't inherit an estate a fraction of the worth of *Javrons* doesn't seem to have deterred her. She believes you have prospects.'

'It doesn't make any sense. I'm convinced I am being manipulated. Arabella Swiffen is stunning. There are any number of suitors she could meet who would be more of a match for her than I ever would.'

Lavinia nodded as she made her way back to her room.

'I warn you sis, if you've made most of this up I'll never forgive you. This is my life we're talking about, not some music hall act from the stage at Drury Lane! Go! Leave me in peace.'

Biting her bottom lip again, Lavinia did as she was bid. She had embellished a little for mischief sake, but her brother's suspicions were not entirely groundless. She also felt they had been invited for a purpose and that Daniel Swiffen, a man that her brother admired – even worshipped – had been less than gallant in the manner in which he had orchestrated this weekend was now becoming more apparent.

Closing the connecting door, she heard Andrew cursing as he fumbled with the studs on his evening shirt.

7

Dinner at *Javrons* that evening was still a formal affair, but at Daniel'sinsistence the atmosphere between the four of them was considerably more relaxed than he could ever imagine his father encouraging. Lavinia had announced, perhaps a little impetuously, that she could play the piano, so over coffee she was urged to do just that, resulting in Arabella forcibly dragging Andrew to his feet to dance with her, although his stiff and uncomfortable demeanour left her feeling slightly angry. Daniel viewed the scene, trying to conceal his amusement. He was convinced his sister was playing Andrew for her own amusement, perhaps because she knew just how uncomfortable he appeared. He lit a cigarette, approaching Lavinia casually he sat beside her on the piano stool.

'I am glad you accepted my invitation. Andrew didn't think you would, and I confess to being pleasantly surprised that you did.'

Lavinia smiled. Her light brown hair was almost blond in the dim light cast by the crimson silk shades of the lamps. 'I almost declined. Andrew didn't seem keen for me to accept and he is *your* friend. Besides, he has formed the impression that my inclusion was merely to distract Arabella in her pursuit of him.'

Daniel smiled. 'Such subterfuge. If that were true it would make me look positively Machiavellian. Besides which, I wanted you to accept as you have been such good company. Vivacious, engaging. Your piano playing has been exquisite. The last time we met at your family home you were still an awkward adolescent, now you are a very beautiful young woman, destined to turn every male head in London I would guess.'

'Excluding those who have already volunteered for – sorry I forget. Talking about the war is banned.'

Daniel smiled, staring into Lavinia's eyes with such intensity it made her blush, so she bowed her head to hide the embarrassment. Then he gently put his finger under her chin and brought her head level with his. 'May I have a cigarette?'

Daniel hesitated, his gaze drifting across to Andrew to check whether his friend had witnessed the moment he had just shared with Lavinia, but she misread the gesture and said, 'If I can accept an invitation to spend a weekend with you without requiring my brother's approval, then surely I can decide for myself when I wish to smoke a cigarette.'

'Of course. Forgive me.' He offered her, his open case and as she put the cigarette between her lips, he took both her hands in his before lighting it for her.

Andrew had softened in his demeanour and was happily twirling Arabella round as they danced. She stopped momentarily, nodding in the direction of their respective siblings. 'What do you think they are conspiring together? Whispering in the corner.'

'Possibly wondering what an undisputed beauty like Arabella Swiffen is doing dancing with a muddle-headed, over sensitive dud like me.'

Arabella looked at him quizzically. He had hoped to say that in a light hearted tone, but could tell from her expression, that he had failed miserably in the attempt. She had never met a man who considered himself less worthy than Andrew Restarick, and she was damned if she was going to indulge him.

'Because many of the *most* eligible bachelors are fighting for King and Country. Why else?'

'Ouch! That comment was unduly harsh!'

'It will teach you not to put yourself down so quickly. Don't underestimate what you're capable of Andrew. From what Daniel has told me, there were enough brutes at Eton willing to denigrate you without you joining in.'

'I suppose I deserve that.' Andrew was determined not to sulk, but he was fazed by Arabella's directness.

'Yes! So stop worrying and dance with me, but not with a look that says your mother has coerced you into it, *because* you want to!'

Andrew nodded, taking Arabella in his arms, he danced with a renewed sense of confidence which came from – he had no idea where – but he was quietly glad for Arabella's censure, because it had given him the jolt he needed to relax and be himself. It also confirmed his earlier belief that she *must* be playing him – for whatever purpose aside from her own amusement he couldn't tell –but he knew that she would never see him as anything other than her brother's friend from Eton, and that as a potential suitor he was out of her league.

While they danced, Lavinia played the piano and Daniel moved closer to her on the narrow stool. His right thigh was touching hers and although she could feel the heat of his flesh, she gave no sign that she was aware of his proximity. He had planned while dressing for dinner that he would see what reaction he could arouse in her, what message his subtle overtures might invoke, and take matters from there. Truth be told he could scarcely remember what Lavinia was like from his visits to Dorset as Andrew liked to dominate his company, as he had little opportunity to do so elsewhere. His friendship with Andrew was still important and he valued it highly, but he couldn't allow himself to be influenced by that if he chose to pursue Lavinia. He was in the market for a wife, not a boon companion, and he wouldn't be diverted from his path.

He had determined that should he receive a positive response from Lavinia and her brother's over-dependence upon him, which still existed, was no deterrent. Andrew would just have to live with it. He had stalled his future long enough. This estate mattered. Its future was integral and the choices he made were key to securing it.

Lavinia had stopped playing and she half rose from the stool until she felt Daniel's hand on hers.

'Viscount Swiffen, please let me go. Are you forgetting your manners?'

'Not at all, but a casual touch between friends can do no harm.'

'I know you are aware of just how fond my brother is of you.'

Daniel coughed, slightly embarrassed by the directness of her words. Andrew had confided to him once that Lavinia understood him better than anyone, aside perhaps from *himself*, and that she accepted him for what he was and whatever it entailed. Regardless of the consequences to her place in society, she had vowed always to *defend* him.

'Your brother was overly dependent upon me – emotionally speaking – at Eton and later at Oxford. He suffered greatly for that dependency at the hands of those who didn't understand the depth of our friendship. I told him firmly that whatever he believed he *felt* for me, could never be encouraged.'

'Do you really think he has accepted that?'

'He has to Lavinia, for both our sakes. Our liberty depends upon it.'

Lavinia nodded slowly. 'Granted, but given how strongly he feels how do you think he will react to any improper conduct by his best friend towards his sister?'

'I can't possibly say as I have no improper conduct in mind.

I confess that I am entranced by you Lavinia Restarick, I will admit to that much. You are enchanting, beautiful!'

Lavinia gulped. She hadn't expected such candour. 'I am going to retire now. Thank you for your hospitality Viscount Swiffen'

Lavinia stood, her gaze fixed upon Daniel. She had the measure of him, or believed she had. He was definitely a complex man, beneath all that aristocratic charm. He could possibly be the most *subtle* game player she had ever met, or was the future Earl Royston possibly considering her as a future wife? How could she ever accept a proposal from him knowing that the brother she *adored* would be devastated beyond endurance?

Daniel took her hand, kissing it with the slightest touch and she saw the intent in his eyes because there was no mistaking it. She was left unnerved, his gaze never left her as she departed the room and Arabella approached Daniel.

'What are you upto?'

'I don't know what you mean.'

'Don't be coy with me. Delightful though she is, that delicate little filly is too candid for her own good. She let it slip earlier that she was invited to distract me from my assiduous pursuit of Andrew, who I can assure you I have no problem resisting despite your assertion to the contrary. Now I find you devoting the entire evening to her. So I repeat what are you up to?'

Daniel smiled his most mischievous smile, dragging on his cigarette so the smoke created a cloud between them he said, 'Do you think she would pass muster with the Old Man?'

'My God! So you are pursuing her? Truth be told as far as our father is concerned any young woman with the right background and a constitution for child bearing, will pass muster! He's become *so* desperate for you to marry and produce a legitimate heir that he's not even demanding whoever she is be a Viscountess in her own right.'

Daniel nodded. 'I do realise I've stalled him for too long.

Olivia Trentham was a good prospect but I was discouraged in my intentions.'

'There is, however, one obvious obstacle to this being a successful plan and that is Andrew. Before tonight I've never been in the arms of a half-decent looking man who couldn't drag his gaze away from my brother.'

Daniel turned his gaze towards Andrew sitting by the fire, silently nursing a Cognac, engrossed in his thoughts, until Arabella approached him. 'Goodnight Andrew. I'm going up so I shall leave you both to your Cognac and non–war talk.'

Andrew stood to take Arabella's hand and kissed it. Arabella smiled at him and left. Daniel had watched the awkward exchange and he was struck by a pang of sudden guilt. He had let Andrew believe Arabella might have been interested in him and the prospect had thrown his friend completely.

When they were alone, Daniel lifted the decanter carrying it over to where Andrew sat. 'I think my sister might be a little disappointed by your lack of response.'

Andrew took a deep breath, rolling the snifter between his hands he said, 'I have been polite, considerate and as engaging as I ever manage to be, but I never promised anything more. I came here for you Daniel!'

'Andrew we have discussed this!'

'I didn't mean in that respect. I'm saying I'm not going to encourage Arabella into thinking my interest in her goes deeper than it does. That would be cruel.'

Daniel was shocked. His conscience piqued because he couldn't claim to have been as honest as his friend. He had manipulated Andrew into this weekend because he wanted to see how the land might lie in respect of Lavinia, and he realised he should have been relieved for Arabella that her feelings for Andrew would never go beyond the platonic, because there was no joy for either to be had there.

'Arabella deserves better than me Daniel. I know she would

admonish me *again* for saying it thus, but it's still the truth.'
Andrew held out his snifter and Daniel refilled it. *He* had been
selfish. Now he needed Lavinia Restarick to accept the proposal
he had determined to make, and to do so swiftly because time
was not on his side. He couldn't afford to be declined a second
time, from the destiny which he knew there was no escape.

December, 1914

The weeks slid by, at a pace which seemed slow to some, but
all too swiftly where Daniel was concerned. In the month since
the weekend with Andrew and Lavinia Restarick at *Javrons*,
Daniel felt as if his feet had barely touched the ground, as
with a ruthlessness he scarcely thought himself capable of,
he had pursued and wooed Lavinia, setting aside all other
considerations, until he was confident of facing his father with
what amounted to an *affait accompli*.

He was going to marry Lavinia Restarick, the sister of an old
friend from Eton, who had been his guest at *Javrons* on several
occasions. The Earl had been astounded, and although he didn't
admit it, verbally, impressed by Daniel's assertiveness, while
Arabella was impressed by how he had so deftly manoeuvred the
situation to his advantage, sweeping Lavinia into a maelstrom
of pre-nuptial excitement and activity, without appearing
to manipulate the situation to the outcome that he had been
planning for all along.

Lavinia's parents were overjoyed that she had accepted the
hand of a future Earl, but Andrew was far from pleased. He
was struggling to come to terms with the speed with which
his friend had moved, and with which his sister had so readily
accepted the proposal, but the reality of having his old friend
from Eton as his future brother-in-law was hardest to take of
all. He was convinced he had been played by Daniel, and that

Lavinia *must* have been in his sights all the time, recalling what Frobisher had said that day at the Club about Olivia Trentham then being the favourite to become Daniel's wife, however, discreet queries he had made since had confirmed to Andrew that Daniel had been refused permission to ask for Olivia's hand. As a result of their meeting, which must, he realised now, have been an enormous slice of good fortune for Daniel, he had turned his attentions to Lavinia and decided her hand in marriage was the prize he *must* win.

Incensed that he had been used by Daniel, Andrew confronted him at his Club on Northumberland Avenue. He had a few Cognacs to boost his courage which proved to be a mistake as it did little to maintain his equilibrium. It was a few days before Christmas, the nuptials would take place on Christmas Eve in the tiny church adjacent to the Swiffen estate.

'Arabella was never remotely infatuated with me, or even mildly interested was she? Lavinia's presence that weekend was never meant as a decoy allowing us the freedom to do as we wished, as you led me to believe. You wanted her there for yourself. Your own selfish ends.'

Daniel was sat with a fellow member that Andrew didn't know, a lieutenant in the same regiment named Martin Fearns, who Andrew had discovered – to add insult-to-injury –had been asked to act as Daniel's best man.

'I apologise if you misunderstood my sister's kindness towards you, Andrew, but she rarely ever shares her infatuations with me. I hate to point out though that you are making quite a fuss.'

Andrew looked around the saloon to see the eyes of several members were fixed on him. 'To hell with them. They should be used to it, having an oaf like Frobisher as a member. Damn you Swiffen! You are marrying my sister in a few days and. I was led to understand somewhat foolishly as it turns out – that you were planning on asking me to act as your best man! So I am guessing that were it ever true, that offer is now withdrawn?'

Daniel, now angered by being the centre of members' attention, stubbed out his cigarette and rising in an fluid movement, took Andrew's arm, but he was shrugged off, at the very moment Frobisher, over imbued with alcohol as usual, appeared.

'You two having a pre-nuptial tiff are you? Never mind Restarick, I am sure that once he's plucked up the courage to deflower the fair Lavinia and done his duty with an heir and spare, he will turn his attentions back onto you.'

Andrew turned and faced Frobisher. 'You dare to insult my sister? You of all people. A lazy pampered boar. A Cognac-sodden inebriate bully, dare to blemish my family name?!'

'Steady on Restarick!. Just a bit of friendly banter.'

'I never was your friend Frobisher. You made sure of that. A fact for which I am now grateful.'

Andrew poked Frobisher in the chest forcibly with his finger, and rocking on his heels, caught off balance, Frobisher fell to the ground. There were guffaws of laughter and shaking of heads as Frobisher struggled getting to his feet, until a steward came to his aid.

'So where are your loyal followers now Frobisher? The ones who so obediently did your bidding at Eton. All deserted you haven't they. Now they can see what a *pathetic* drunk you really are!'

Daniel put a hand on Andrew's arm, but it was shrugged off and with that Andrew left. He would have liked to stay and settle the score with Daniel as well, but he couldn't trust himself not to be overwrought and betray him. He realised that despite everything that had unfolded in recent weeks, he still cared too much for Daniel to bring such trouble on both their heads. Besides Frobisher was right. He was *jealous* of Daniel marrying Lavinia, because he knew he didn't love her. She was a means to an end, and she would doubtless discover that in due course, but by then it would be too late, because she would be Daniel's wife, and all *his* efforts to dissuade her from accepting Daniel's proposal these last few weeks, will have amounted to nothing.

In four days' time, Daniel would be bound to him through marriage as they had once been bound in friendship. Where that friendship stood now, he had no idea. However they progressed from this night onwards, Andrew was certain that he could never trust Daniel Swiffen as he once had *so* unswervingly.

Javrons Estate – Christmas Eve, 1914

Daniel looked out onto the crisp frost-covered lawn, of the estate and allowed a brief smile to cross his lips. He had even surprised himself with the decisive swiftness with which he had acted to become engaged to Lavinia Restarick, and how she had acquiesced to the suggestion that their engagement should be a short one, without him having to place any emphasis on the imperative for their nuptials to be conducted with urgency. Although a pre-Christmas wedding suited him fine, he had made it look as if it had been her idea. The problem with Andrew's reluctance to accept the marriage did darken the mood, and he knew she would be upset if he followed through with the thinly-veiled threat not to attend the ceremony. He felt he had been left with no choice, about seeking someone else as his best man, and although Stephen Trentham would have been the obvious choice, Daniel realised, he had to accept some guilt for allowing that friendship to slide. He had come to realise there was a lot of reparation ahead of him in healing friendships that he had allowed to lapse, but he was satisfied that finally he had done what was expected. He had fulfilled his duty to the estate. He had found himself a wife, now to sire an heir so that when the call to arms came, it would leave only his fear of military action, to which he freely admitted, to overcome.

There was a slight knock on the bedroom door and he gave the command to enter his suite. Martin Fearns appeared, an ironic smile on his face.

'How is the groom feeling?'

'Nervous. Apprehensive. Wondering what the hell I am doing!'

'Well that covers a lot. Relax Daniel. You've picked a beautiful bride, who is going to do you proud as the Viscountess Swiffen. From what I have seen, she is engagingly vivacious. Nobody is going to struggle to recognise this as a genuine love match.'

Daniel shook his head slightly. 'Aside from those who know me well.'

'So you're referring to the brother who made such a show of himself at the Club? Is he coming today?'

'I don't know. Lavinia wants him there so for her sake, I hope that he does. It will look odd on the Restarick side, as it's known how close they are. Although that's the least of my concerns. It's the other compelling priority of this whole sorry mess! The consummation to put it crudely. You'll think me terribly *gauche*, but I'm woefully inexperienced.'

Martin Fearns fiddled with his cap, laughing nervously. He bowed his head blushing. 'I recall were you never quite adventurous when it came to romantic liaisons.'

Daniel shook his head slowly, laughing. 'Is that what you called them? Come on, don't be coy. There's nothing especially romantic about visiting a house of ill-repute.'

Daniel led his friend to the table on which a tray with coffee stood. 'Help yourself. I need some air.'

'You want company?' asked Fearns.

Daniel shook his head.

By midday the church bells were ringing and Daniel stood at the altar waiting for his bride. Martin Fearns stood at his side.

Stephen Trentham had sent a telegram politely declining his invitation, citing pressure of work at the Foreign Office and he *still* couldn't be certain that the bride's brother would attend. It was all such a goddamned mess. A shambles!

Half-turning he looked at the family pews where his father sat smiling. At least someone was happy with proceedings. The Old Man had won. The unbroken line of succession would be kept intact, if only he could consummate the marriage swiftly, or else manage once he had answered the call to arms not to – using his father's choice of words – "*Get his bloody head shot off.*"

Lavinia Restarick was a beautiful bride. Both her soon to be sisters-in-law thought as much, standing behind her in the Grand Hall at *Javrons*. This was it, Lavinia thought, despite all the pre-marriage nerves, the earnest attempts by Andrew to dissuade her from accepting the proposal, and his barely concealed disappointment when their parents had given both their consent for her to be asked, and the marriage their blessing. She looked up at her father smiling thinly. 'Andrew? Has he come?'

All she got was a shrug of the shoulders and then a light encouraging squeeze of her arm as the footman opened the front door and the highly polished black landau carriage bearing the Swiffen coat of arms shone in the weak December sunlight as it stood waiting for her. Random snowflakes began to fall and Lavinia smiled, although she felt the tears welling.

'As a girl I dreamed of a Christmas wedding. I can't help thinking what it must be like in the trenches this Christmas. All those brave young men, some of them still only boys. Far from home. To think they genuinely believed it would all be over by now.'

'Shh. This is your day to shine. Think happy thoughts. Selfish ones even.'

The bridesmaids nodded approvingly, as Lavinia looked at her father nodding silently, he gave her arm another squeeze and they stepped forward as she went to seal her destiny as the Viscountess Swiffen.

She didn't see Andrew among the congregation until after they had exchanged vows, the register had been signed, and she was walking out of the church on Daniel's arm as his wife. She had *hoped* her brother would come, and yet she had also feared that as the vicar asked if there was any legal impediment to the marriage he would step forward. Thankfully he hadn't, but he stood at the back with his fists clenched as they left the church.

At the reception afterwards he kept his distance as Lavinia did the rounds among the assembled guests. He had decided on the journey he had taken alone from London not to do anything rash that would ruin his sister's day and embarrass his family. The prospect of ostracism didn't sit well with him, but he'd determined to confront Daniel the first chance he got.

'So you came to see your sister happily married after all?' asked Daniel pointedly.

'I wouldn't go as far as that.'

'Look at her Andrew. Doesn't she look radiant to you?'

'For the time being, yes. Until you receive the call to arms and she wakes each day to the very real prospect of widowhood. Or maybe once she has done her duty by you as a wife and mother for your precious heirs, and having exhausted your use of her you'll return to your old ways. Your *"proclivities"* as Trentham liked to refer to them. I should know better than most. Where is the esteemed Trentham today? I thought he would be here, as watching your back was always his primary role in life.'

Daniel moved to strike Andrew, but he had moved away and the crystal Champagne flute fell crashing to the floor. As startled guests looked in his direction, he laughed nervously. 'I would have thought any wedding day nerves I had would have come before the ceremony. I trust you were not hurt Andrew?'

Andrew looked intently at Daniel and all the emotions

he had felt on first meeting him at Eton came flooding back. Daniel challenged him with his look and Andrew, turning away, smiled. 'Not at all. No harm done.'

Andrew, smiling, walked away, to mingle with other guests, but Daniel was left in no doubt of the menacing intent in his voice.

★ ★ ★

Daniel nursed a brandy snifter on his knee by the roaring fire in his bedroomsuite as he waited patiently – and with trepidation – for Lavinia to join him. He took a large gulp of Cognac to settle his nerves and then there was a knock at the door. He expected a footman, or maybe the maid who had been assigned to look after Lavinia, but it was Andrew who opened the door.

'Do you mind?' he asked.

'I should, but I doubt you would take the hint Andrew, so whatever it is you have to say, *please* be brief.'

'I want you to acknowledge to me at least, that you manipulated my sister into marrying you. That she is an expedient means to an end. Nothing more.'

Daniel stood to face him and suddenly he saw a hint of intimidation in Andrew's demeanour, as if he felt threatened.

'So what is it you imagine, I will do once I've sired my heir and spare? Discard her. Humiliate her with my indiscretions?'

Andrew averted his gaze from his friend's scrutiny, because he knew what he was asking of Daniel was unreasonable and undeliverable.

'I've never thought until today Andrew, what a weak and self-indulgent fool you are! As we stand here in the warmth of my bedroom suite, discussing my ability to remain faithful to my marriage vows, there are men, some younger than us, freezing in the trenches in France and wondering if tomorrow, Christmas Day, will be their last twenty-four hours!

'Men of our generation cannot plan ahead Andrew. This bloody war has seen to that. It was supposed to be over by now. Victory before Christmas! Do you remember that? You also may have to face the reality of the trenches very soon. I hope not, for your sake, but it's possible. I'll admit I'm bloody scared, to you– anyone in private–although it's not what is expected of us. The privileged class!

With the stiff upper lip. So why don't you quit the self-pity and wake up to the bloody reality of the hell that we're in?'

Andrew, turning away, flinched slightly. All his courage, bolstered by several Cognacs had deserted him now. He sounded and thought he must have looked a desperate man.

'So to answer your question: no, I didn't set out to manipulate Lavinia into marriage, any more than I did to Olivia Trentham, but my responsibilities – my obligations – have always been different to yours. Have you thought for one moment that when you were trying so very hard to dissuade her from accepting my proposal, that *if* she had wanted to, all she had to do was decline?'

Andrew choking back on a sob turned away and Daniel embarrassed, finished his Cognac in a gulp. He looked at his friend who was now also his brother-in-law, hoping to show compassion, but he felt revulsion. He had always known Andrew to be over-dependant and emotional, but this was the worst he had seen him.

Daniel turned back to look at Andrew, struggling to keep the pity out of his tone. 'I think you should leave now before *my* bride returns.'

The emphasis that he placed on the word *my* was intended as a barb and Andrew took it as such. Shaking his head, he said. 'I'll never forget how close we were at Eton, even though you have chosen to deny it. What we meant to each other. What you *still* mean to me.'

'No! Not this again. You agreed we would never speak of it.'

'I didn't agree really, it was what Trentham led you to believe, having *coerced* me into accepting his version of how things should proceed. Because he always believed he knew best.'

Daniel's face was like thunder, as he took two steps towards a retreating Andrew. 'That is because he *did* on that occasion. Now get out!'

Andrew looked at Daniel and he saw in his eyes something he had never expected to see, revulsion. Shocked, he rocked back on his heels and fled.

What neither of them knew was that Lavinia, planning to surprise her husband, by entering the marital suite via the bathroom that connected their bedrooms, had on hearing the raised voices of her husband and her brother, paused at the door and she overheard almost everything. Gasping with shock, she stifled the cry, forcing down the sudden feeling of nausea which assailed her. She whispered to herself, 'Andrew and Daniel? It can't be.'

She had arrived at the door mid-conversation, but she had seen enough in the looks exchanged between them. The disgust of her husband, clashing with the hurt etched into Andrew's features, and the reality dawned on her. She couldn't be sure whether some of it was self-disgust at himself, that Daniel was expressing, or only at Andrew, but it was earth-shattering just the same. Her brother had confessed other such infatuations to her before, because she was the only person he could trust to confide in, but she never believed his infatuations had ever involved intimacy, given the risk involved. Now suddenly all *his* reservations about her marrying Daniel made sense. It hadn't all been a reaction motivated by jealousy, to a crush that had been rebuffed. She could still be judging her husband unduly harshly without being aware of all the facts, but how could she establish them without letting him know what she had heard?

The undeniable reality was though, that if what she had heard contained even a kernel of truth, then she would have to face that in church, before God, she had promised to be faithful to what amounted to a lie, and thus made the biggest mistake of her life.

8

Covington, Devon – December, 1914

The green sloping hills around Covington had vanished beneath a blanket of snow, as had any lingering hopes that victory would come swiftly, and for Laura Weston, the possibility that her beloved Alex would escape the horror of the trenches.

As Christmas approached he was the last man under the age of thirty still left in the print room at the *Covington Echo* and the paper's proprietors, while grateful for his loyalty, approached him to express their concern, *urging* him to consider his duty to King and Country, as so many of the apprentice typesetters and junior reporters had already done.

There was a weekly roll-call to acknowledge the former staff who had already lost their lives and each time Alex was left feeling more guilty, reddening with embarrassment as the whispers around him grew louder.

There had been some residual awkwardness between him and Laura following the incident with the white feather, but he had assumed the role of peacemaker, and having accepted George Weston's invitation to Christmas lunch, he knew that to enjoy the day in an ambient atmosphere he would 'tough' it out' until after Christmas.

On Christmas morning he arrived at the station master's cottage to find George in good spirits. He had extended the invitation to include Effie Conyer, but Alex hadn't been surprised when his mother declined, as he knew when she had a new love interest in her life; she had even less attention to pay him, and although a tinge of guilt gnawed at him he felt relieved when she had said no.

Laura called to them as she placed the last dishes on the table and Alex could see the effort that she had gone to; even though she mentioned the feast would be satisfactory rather than lavish; he was about to remark that it was better than what the troops could expect, missing the sly shake of George's head.

'You're not ruining my day with war talk,' she commanded in a broad Devon burr that forbade defiance. George smiled lightly, thinking how much she now sounded and behaved like her mother, in so many facets of her character with each passing day. Despite Laura's protests, George had felt obliged to also invite Stoughton, as he had once been on Christmas Day duty as a junior porter, but they had all been relieved when Stoughton had dismissively declined in his customary sneering fashion, even though he had derided a sadistic pleasure from goading Laura into thinking that he would accept, and how much she might enjoy having him and Conyer vying for her affections over lunch. She was heartily grateful that it was just the three of them as a few of Covington's womenfolk had warned her against extending an invitation to Effie Conyer who she had been told could be quite nasty in her cups, when her latest relationship broke down, which everyone aside from her could foresee would be the likely outcome, the moment it began.

Laura had on numerous occasions expressed her sympathy to Alex for the scorn his mother brought on herself and by turns on him, but he had told her firmly that he didn't want her sympathy in that regard and he never would. While Laura had been resentful when he had relayed the *Echo's* concerns about him not having volunteered, saying it was just their reputation as employers that was motivating them. Although he kept his counsel, he had decided for himself to volunteer in the New Year, vowing that this time he would not be swayed from his course. There was no immediate prospect as far as he could see of the Government introducing nationwide conscription, compelling every man below a certain age to fight. He had his own reasons for holding back, but he'd decided that he would take the censure of his elders in the print room at the *Echo* no longer, albeit still conscious of those he would be leaving behind.

Casualty Clearing Station, – France

Eloise Chagall was beginning to feel as much like a Red Cross nurse as she had looked the part from the moment she first wore the uniform, shortly after leaving Paris. She hadn't any idea about what she was going to do as she had walked from the de Valois mansion, but she had been certain she couldn't remain in the capital. She would always associate the city with her relationship with Etienne, thus it brought only painful memories, so the Red Cross provided her an opportunity for escape and the chance to do some good. She would immerse herself in the lives of brave soldiers and however mundane the duties were, she could hope that by tending to the wounded and homesick volunteers who came into her care, for however brief a time, and in offering solace where it was needed, would help her to assuage the pain which lodged in her heart after Etienne's rejection.

At the start she had given little consideration for her own safety, not caring if her fate was to die in some field hospital close to the front. She was seen, she knew by her colleagues, as cold and aloof, but she didn't care about that either. She was here to do a vital job like them. They didn't need to know how raw she was inside. That her heart had been broken and she never expected to love again as strongly as she had for de Valois, with the knowledge like a corrosive pain in her stomach that whatever pleasures, he had been happy to take from her in the bedroom, she had never in his eyes ever been good enough to become his wife. She hadn't allowed herself to think how she might react; were he brought wounded into the CCS. Could she absolve herself from treating him or would that mean having to reveal her story, and thus give him more prominence in her present, when she had vowed to leave him in the past? Mercifully, she had been spared that ordeal, but there were countless others who came into her care, whose wounds were extensive enough to realise that it was on a knife edge whether they could survive; whose stories they were eager to share, which had the power to tug at the heart, even one as bruised as hers. Whatever her colleagues felt about her they couldn't accuse her of not caring for the patients, and her instinctive compassion which had come from where she knew not, had been noticed and commended upon.

When Sister Hopkins first brought the claims that she craved solitude, and that the other nurses felt they couldn't rely on her, Eloise refuted the claims strongly, which didn't meet the Sister's approval. Although when challenged the Sister couldn't point to any example where Eloise had been neglectful in her duties. That when her colleagues needed to rely on her she would prove herself more than worthy and at that point the Sister had dismissed her. The meeting had left Eloise feeling angry and resentful, but it was the plight of one private who helped to soothe her anger. She had heard him in his bed, singing the carol. *O Come, All Ye Faithful,"* but his voice sounded weak, reedy and full of pent-up emotion, and when she approached him she saw tears welling in his eyes.

The carol service had been the idea of the medical-officer

who saw it as a morale boost, although she had initially been dismissive, huffing silently at the absurdity of it. She couldn't see how singing carols could possibly boost the morale of a nineteen-year-old boy away from home at Christmas, wounded in a temporary hospital. Private Parrish had been singing loudly with the others at first, but as Eloise approached the emotion overcame him and he was choked, his voice faltering until he couldn't be heard at all, and she took her handkerchief and gently brushed away the tears. His lips began to tremble when he attempted to thank her, so instead she lit one of his cigarettes, placing it between his lips. She lay a hand on his shoulder and began singing with him, and then smiling she moved away until she felt his grip tighten on her arm. 'Don't leave me nurse.'

'I have other patients,' she said gently, but firmly, and he smiled removing his arm. He wasn't singing anymore, but the voices of other fitter patients could still be heard. Soon they would return to the Front to face whatever fate had in store for them. They moved onto the next carol and she leaned over Parrish and gently pressed her lips to his. She hoped nobody could see but she didn't care. There would be others like Parrish whose story would get into her too deeply and she guessed that might be another cause to sanction her.

'I shall come back, when I can, but please no more tears.' She left him with her brightest smile but had she looked in the direction of the office, she would have seen that Sister Hopkins, had witnessed the scene with Private Parrish, and as Eloise moved on the Sister inclined her head, allowing a slight smile to touch the corners of her mouth.

At the end of her shift, Eloise was summoned back to Sister Hopkins' office and she could tell from the slight smile on the Sister's face that she was not being recalled for another chastisement. The Sister, a woman who had dedicated herself to a career in the nursing profession and would continue within it, once the war was over, could be described as having a face, that would be remembered rather than being admired as overly attractive, and if she was jealous of Eloise's exceptional beauty she was sufficiently professional not to show it.

'I happened to notice how especially kind you were to Private Parrish. He found telling his family that he wouldn't be home for Christmas, particularly hard. He is a very troubled young man, one of many I'm afraid, and although his physical injuries are not too extensive that he shouldn't recover, his mental state is currently very fragile, however, I am keen to urge caution upon you. It wouldn't do to over indulge him. Your approach was appropriate and I'm impressed.'

'Mercí Sister, but I think…'

'Go on.'

'The carol singing was making him feel sad. Reminding him of home.'

'So you chose to comfort him?' Sister Hopkins nodded, adding, 'I believe you were not convinced by the benefits of a carol concert to boost morale.' Eloise blushed slightly and bowed her head.

'For what it is worth, I'm inclined to agree – but that doesn't go beyond this room. That being said our role is to fix their wounds so they can be sent on to the Field Hospital for further treatment or sent back into action. The hierarchy are struggling to keep morale up, especially now. After all, most of the young men who volunteered these last few months were allowed to believe it would be over by now. That victory would be swift and they would be celebrating it and enjoying Christmas at home. Sadly that myth was allowed to gain hold and last too long. I always feared the war would last longer.'

'So the likes of Private Parrish will be patched up and sent back to fight before they are ready and a few carols are supposed to lift their spirits?'

'Nurse Chagal, let me remind you the men's morale is their commanding officer's responsibility, and if the power to veto such an event is beyond my authority, then it is certainly above yours. From what I have seen and read of his report, men like Parrish were ill-equipped to cope with the demands of the Front before he was injured – and is even less so now – however, his fate lies in the hands of the MO and *his* CO.'

Sister Hopkins sat down and taking a deep breath she considered for a moment. 'I have to say I am somewhat disappointed. I called for you to express how I was impressed by your conduct, yet once again you have managed to demonstrate your reluctance to respect authority. You do appear to be aloof from your colleagues which is regrettable. My position demands I keep a distance, as it enables me to discipline objectively. You have no such restrictions and yet, again and again, I receive comments that you are too distant, and as such they don't trust you.'

'I fulfil my duties to my ability Sister. I am here to care for the patients not to win a prize for being the most popular nurse. What is the point of forming attachments Sister, when the next twenty-four hours could be my last, or theirs. I learnt the hard way Sister that to give yourself too freely brings only pain.'

Sister Hopkins considered her a moment. She had never doubted that Nurse Chagal had soul or the capacity for passion, she just thought her too controlled to let it show.

'He hurt you that much did he?'

'I never said, what I felt had anything to do with a man?'

'Didn't you?'

Eloise bowed her head, realising she had said too much. For months she had kept her counsel, not allowed what her colleagues thought about her, to matter, so why let her guard down now? With Sister Hopkins of all people.

'May I go Sister?'

Sister Hopkins nodded watching as Eloise left. She had seen so many nurses come through under her authority both at the London Hospital and here at the Front. Usually by the time they had been trained and were ready to move on, she had some idea of what motivated them, where their strengths lie and *their* weaknesses. She had seen something of both in Eloise Chagal, and yet she still believed the surface had barely been scratched. She had the potential to be a very good nurse, but the lacerating pain she felt, which Sister Hopkins knew could only be the product of a broken heart, could ultimately destroy her unless Nurse Chagal could find it within herself to forgive. She looked down at the personal file and was tempted to record some comment on their encounter, but she demurred. Having seen how she had dealt with Private Parrish she would let the disregard for authority go this time, but she had her on notice. Even so, as she closed the file and replaced it, she was sorely tempted to whisper, 'What a waste.'

Covington, Devon – Christmas Day

After lunch, which had been beautifully prepared by Laura, George Weston decided it was time for a stroll, so grabbing his pipe, he chewed on it reflectively, smiling encouragingly at Alex as he left. This was his moment and although George didn't know exactly what the boy had in mind, he knew it involved Laura and that his daughter knew her mind, knew what she wanted and that her world revolved around Alex Conyer, and that was how it should be. *He* was still a significant presence in her life as her father, because for so long it had just been the two of them. Whatever plans the boy was hatching could only be temporary and Laura was slowly becoming accustomed to that reality, having valiantly fought against it for months.

The incident of the woman with the white feathers had hurt her to the core, but the strength of Alex's reaction had shocked her most. Through the frosted scullery window, he saw Alex putting an arm around Laura's shoulder. He was a good young man. More than a credit to his mother than Effie, deserved, but every inch the measure of what he would expect a grandson of Ben Conyer, to be. George remembered Alex's maternal grandfather, who the boy had idolised, as a solid honest decent stoker on the Great Western Railways, who might have hoped Alex would follow him, but George was certain, nodding his approval that he would have no hesitation in giving his blessing to a marriage when the time was right, and that he couldn't have hoped for a better prospect for his only child if he had picked Alex Conyer himself.

'Was my father trying to be discreet?' Laura asked, her green eyes dancing merrily.

'I wouldn't know. Although it's his custom to light his pipe and go for a stroll after dinner isn't it?'

'Yes dinner, not lunch. Don't be evasive with me Alex Conyer. Haven't you got something you need to ask?' Laura said in her broad Devon burr, eyeing him suspiciously.

'You know that will come when the time is right, but I wanted you to know I'm going to volunteer. I have to do this Laura, once the year is out.'

'You have to tell me this on Christmas Day?' She was overwhelmed by it, but kept her tone neutral.

'We've been avoiding the issue of when I would have to enlist for weeks. I wanted to tell you, before someone saw me coming out of the recruitment office and I've not made a decision about when as yet. I wanted you to have time to come to terms with it.'

Laura knew that she probably never would come to terms with the reality of it. There were tears streaming down her cheeks now and she savagely wiped them away.

'I thought you were working up to a proposal?'

'Hey you're still the only girl for me Laura Weston!'

'You still want that then?'

'Of course.' He let his thumb pad trace her tears, pushing

them aside. Laura shook her head, backing away. Now the prospect of losing him seemed more real than ever, and so she dare not let him close. She felt the brass fender of the fire against the back of her legs, the heat of it. She wiped at her tears with her apron, and Alex looked at her bewildered and confused.

'I think you should leave now. You've had your Christmas feast, so leave me be. I've nothing else to offer you today.'

'Laura!' he pleaded, striding towards her, arms outstretched.

'Just go Alex!' she shrieked and he went without another word, without a backward glance at her one more time, but had he done so he would have seen that Laura had fled.

Javrons – Hertfordshire, New Year's Eve, 1914

Daniel stood at the tall window of his bedroom suite looking down at the curving gravel driveway and the frost-covered manicured lawns beyond. He was waiting with growing impatience for his wife to heed the call to see him, but Lavinia was not herself. She had been ill at ease and moody since their wedding night and he had no idea why.

Their first attempts at making love had met with disaster, although he attached as much blame for that on his shoulders. She was withdrawn from him emotionally and to some extent physically, although she had done her duty by him in that respect, it had been like a resigned surrender that this was the fate she had chosen for herself and now she would have to repent. It was if the bright vivacious girl he had proposed to; had vanished from the moment he had placed the ring on her finger, and he was impatient in demanding his *right* to know why. The connecting door opened gently and she stood there, head turned to one side, her eyes sunken. Maybe she was feeling ill, but all his queries to her in that regard had been met with a shake of her head. She could still look divine with hair falling onto her shoulders, and a slight smile lighting her eyes.

'So you got my message? Unnecessary had you not seen the need to keep that door locked!' He had rehearsed the scenario in his mind while he had waited, and he had decided to be amenable, but now he couldn't keep the sarcasm from his voice.

Lavinia shook her head wearily. 'I'm tired Daniel and I *didn't* feel upto fulfilling my wifely duties this morning, now, however, I feel amenable having bathed, I feel refreshed, although I detect the petulance in your tone, like a small boy whose had his favourite toy taken away.'

'Strange as it may seem, my interest in you does extend beyond the physical demands of our marriage and your presence in the marital bed. I have received my call-up papers. The Hertfordshire Regiment requires my services at the Front. It has been inevitable, and yet I was – am *still* dreading it!'

Lavinia turned to face him, pouting mockingly. 'Still afraid of having to fight are you?

'Not afraid. Apprehensive.'

'Face upto it Daniel. You were never meant to be a man of action. Something else you have in common with my brother Andrew.'

Daniel pursed his lips. Lavinia was in the mood to goad him and he was equally determined to resist her provocation. She had left the sash of her robe undone and he could see the length of her thighs, which had been wrapped around him during sex. He wished he could make love to her; as she deserved to be. That he could enjoy his conjugal rights instead of seeing them merely as a dutiful by-product of their marriage, so that he could sire an heir. Now the reality of his call-up had heightened the urgency, and yet he lacked the impetus to force the situation to bring his wife to the pinnacle of her sexual desire, and to lose himself inside her. He could imagine the mocking taunts of his peers who had regularly frequented the brothels of the West End and had goaded him into joining them. How they would have appreciated Lavinia for the beautiful woman she was, without for a moment agonising over the emotional impact of it. Yet that was what he had courted and married her for wasn't it? All in a matter of weeks, and in such a single-minded manner that he had sacrificed another valued friendship and all in the pursuit of his cursed, bloody duty.

'What's the matter Daniel, don't you want me? In view of what you summoned me to your bedroom to tell me, I would have thought that sealing the deal and siring your heir would have become even more urgent.'

He clenched his clammy fists at his side and approached her, as she moved to him alluringly, determined to taunt and tease him as her thigh touched his and he felt he was on fire. Whatever lust she provoked in him was heightened to an unbearable level and he felt himself losing control. Of needing her, more than he had ever wanted, or was prepared to admit, and that would give her a power in the dynamic of their marriage, that he wasn't certain he could concede and still be the man he knew himself to be. It shocked him to realise she didn't leave him feeling cold. She had fired his imagination with the strength of her sensuality and she basked in seeing how he reacted to the sensual power, that she was excited to exert.

He was confident, however, that she would never claim his heart and deep in his soul, he despised himself for that, almost as much as he could her for the carnal instincts she provoked, and for herself Lavinia knew she held a trump card, because her husband had no idea, she had overheard the conversation with her brother. That Andrew's infatuation with Daniel hadn't always been so one-sided, that he had reciprocated once and might have done so again had Stephen Trentham not intervened. The grim reality was that her husband of less than a week, was a fraud and she had paid a heavy price for not seeing that before he had placed the ring on her finger, so she would punish him with her feminine desires and her wanton ways, knowing that however much he tried to show how he desired her, he couldn't commit.

'You can't help wanting to desire me, as a man should desire his wife, but it isn't there *is* it Daniel? There is something missing.'

'Don't taunt me Lavinia. I refuse to be ensnared by your futile attempts to expose any weakness you presume that I have.'

'I don't presume anything Daniel, I know what it is you want, what you surrendered to at Eton, with all the risk it involved, even though it only happened once. Andrew isn't here and you've surrendered his friendship as well, in pursuit of what you need to be. What your father, the Earl, demands that you show yourself as. This legacy you have strived against your whole life.'

Daniel backed away, rocking on his heels. Lavinia was smiling at him, but it wasn't the smile of a devoted loving wife. It was the smile of a temptress, who had, should she ever choose to use it, the power to destroy him.

He reached out as if to touch her and she shrank back. 'I don't know what you believe you know my darling wife, but remember we exchanged our vows to love and honour, a week ago, so whatever misdeed you are alluding to, we shall never speak of it again. Understand?'

He held her face in his hand nodding, waiting for her acquiescence and Lavinia nodded. She had seen for the first time a hint of the man her husband could be if provoked, and she wasn't too proud to admit that it scared and excited her at the same time.

Daniel reached out and gently he pulled her towards him, kissing her on the lips, devouring her mouth. Kisses that were hotly passionate and intended to punish her, as equally as they were to arouse. He pushed her down onto the bed and removing her robe, ran his trembling hands upto her breasts. She smiled as this was the level of passion that she had hoped to unleash inside him all week, but it had been sadly missing from their clumsy attempts to sire an heir. She realised she may never claim his love, but she had proved she could make him *want* her, and that was a weakness she planned to exploit.

9

The tension which had grown between Alex and Laura didn't stop them trying to make Christmas special – as Alex had pointed out as subtly as he could that so many of his generation were not so fortunate to be spending it with their loved ones – but it increased as the last days of the old year slid by, giving way to the new, and taking with it the optimism which had been rife in the golden days of late summer but was nothing but a memory now.

There was only hope that an end to hostilities was close, and into this atmosphere Alex took the required steps to enlist. His decision brought relief at the *Echo*, but Laura was still struggling, and knew she would until the moment came for him to go, then her anger and resentment would turn to missing him, but the inevitability of his going, never quite sat easily upon her shoulders.

George knew it was best to keep his distance when Laura's *ire* was at its height and advised his head porter to do the same, but with Stoughton's appetite for stirring trouble, he ignored the advice and felt the full force of Laura's wrath. For his part George had almost abandoned hope of having his head porter replaced, and he became more convinced that Stoughton must have the 'goods' on someone at head office who was compelled to protect him, why else would they put up with such an insolent and lazy employee? 'What your lass needs is a *man* to take her in hand. She's got plenty of spirit, I'll say that for her, but it's wasted on a boy like Conyer.'

'Even if she were interested, I'd have my reservations, however, as Laura *loathes* you Stoughton as much as I do, if not more so, I have no need to worry. Now get back to work, there are passengers requiring assistance.'

George clamped his pipe between his teeth, sneering as Stoughton retreated back and turning his attention to the paperwork in front of him, he reflected on the fact that he couldn't have been more worried if he'd had a son with a decision like the one Alex was having to make. He was the centre of Laura's world and he wasn't sure how his lass could cope, should Alex fail to return.

The Swiffen House – Cavendish Square

Daniel regretted the confrontation with Lavinia from the moment, he allowed himself to lose control. Even being tempted to raise his hand had been unforgivable, and he had promised never do so again, but what was equally regrettable was giving her false hope that they might enjoy anything resembling a normal marriage. He was very fond of her, but he wasn't in love with her, but the arrival of his call-up papers from the regiment that three generations of Swiffen men had served, had altered everything, and the urgency with which he now wished to sire an heir had increased. He dressed in his regimental uniform and stood admiring himself in the cheval mirror. He looked like a soldier, but could he stand any chance of being one, with the fears he held about going into action? Lavinia entered his suite with a smile and mischievously; at the sight of him, she said caustically, 'How dashing.' He ignored her barb. She only came to his suite; when summoned and always with one purpose in mind because she had no delusions about her marriage now. She had her brother to thank for the candour she would never have received from her husband.

She had invented an excuse of needing to be in London with Daniel when he attended his Regimental HQ, and in a tiny restaurant, she had 'bullied' the truth out of Andrew about his friendship with Daniel, and while she accepted her brother's assurance that the initial infatuation had been *his,* she knew despite everything, Daniel had led her to believe, that eventually the attraction had been mutual.

'Don't you comprehend the enormity of the risk you were both taking?' she asked. There was a deliberate edge to her tone and she didn't care that he blanched at it, although determined not to blub in public, Andrew bit his bottom lip and nodded silently.

'The risk might have been even greater for Daniel, given his family's position and the title he would inherit, at least that's the way Trentham always saw it.'

'That doesn't excuse him laying the blame for it at you! Even so that is why Daniel has denied you ever since, and why you were quarrelling with him on my wedding night?'

Lavinia nodded as realisation struck her brother. 'I overheard almost every word and Daniel is right about one thing: exposure would spell social ruin for all of us. Potentially imprisonment for you both. I would be outcast. An *object* of pity!'

'Is he aware that you know everything?'

Lavinia shook her head, hoping Andrew was too upset to be intuitive. Flat denial had been Daniel's tactic during their quarrel and she was happy to leave it at that.

'He's received the call from his regiment, confirming that he will be going to France and he's terrified. Convinced it's *his* fate to be killed in action. It's what the Earl has believed all along. So it's all about the future now for my in-laws – the next generation – so I dread what their reaction would be should I give birth to a girl.'

'Are you expecting?' Andrew asked, hoping his tone sounded neutral.

'Not as yet, but it's only a matter of time. At least then I will have fulfilled my obligations. Haven't you found anyone to take you on yet? Hasn't one of those numerous young ladies mother is *so* keen to pair you off with passed muster? The sister of some old Etonian?'

Andrew shook his head in revulsion at the idea. 'No thank God. Imagine having to consummate with someone you feel absolutely nothing for. I would sooner remain a bachelor.'

Lavinia pulled a face as she sipped her coffee. 'Please Andrew spare me the self-pity. I am locked into a loveless marriage to Daniel, which I might have been spared had you spoken up sooner.'

'I *implored* with him not to trifle with your emotions. Definitely not to propose,because I felt sure you would accept. Don't forget you were quite dazzled by the idea of becoming the Viscountess Swiffen!'

Lavinia put down her cup with a slight clatter, ignoring the irritated looks of other patrons and stifled a gasp. 'I accept that it's not all your fault. I was swept off my feet by the whirlwind courtship and his proposal. Then hearing the two of you made my blood run cold'

'We were fortunate it was Stephen Trentham that came into Daniel's rooms that morning and found us, and although Daniel would deny it as a matter of course, I am convinced that is why Trentham refused to be his best man, because he might have suspected the marriage could be used as a ruse for Daniel and me to start seeing each other, and then all his good work at Eton would have been wasted.'

Andrew threw Lavinia a sharp look and she smiled. 'All a

bit elaborate isn't it? Besides I thought Trentham was incensed by Daniel's attempt to court his cousin Olivia. Don't look so alarmed. I realised I wasn't Daniel's first choice.'

Andrew took her gloved hand in his, squeezing it tight. 'I'm sorry Vin truly, but if I had put more effort into deterring you from accepting Daniel's proposal would you have heeded my warnings or resented me for trying to spoil things for you?'

If Lavinia was surprised by his use of childhood pet name, she didn't show it. Sipping her coffee she shrugged. 'Perhaps not. Daniel saw to it that I had every reason to accept him. I married in haste, at his behest and now I am to repent. So be it. Conceiving a child is essential and it will make a difference. As will the war, but either way this is my lot now, for better or worse.'

Covington, Devon

The days turned to weeks and still Alex waited. His life held in abeyance and although Laura had come round to the reality that he was going, she struggled to accept the possibilities that may come with it: that very soon she would be stood at the scullery window, expecting his arrival and realising that he wasn't coming for dinner because he was far away in France, fighting in a war, they been allowed to believe would be over now; fighting the enemy and *hoping* to survive.

When his papers came, he was more resigned than anything else. He lacked the sense of optimism with which so many of his peers had volunteered, but then that had been in the early days of the war, and when they believed all the hype.

Now opinion had become jaded and as Christmas had come and gone with no victory in sight, the consensus was for it just to be over, and whenever it came, couldn't be soon enough.

He had suggested they should spend his last night in

Covington together. Out of respect for her father he booked a room above the *Covington Arms*. There he would consummate his love for Laura Weston for the first time, and he would make it special. For anything else he couldn't make promises, and that was the truth neither was prepared to confront.

They walked out of the cottage, hand in hand down the hill into town. The twilight of a cold February evening chilled their bones. The hills surrounding the town were still deep in snow, the dry-stone walls were laden with it, but as winter held its grip they were cocooned in their own world for tonight at least. In the muted candlelit room, she looked more beautiful than ever to him, her green eyes dancing eagerly with anticipation of what was to come. It was the first night she hadn't slept under her father's roof, and the enormity of it wasn't lost on her as it was in many respects the *most* important night of her life. For his part Alex had never *coerced* her into taking their relationship further in the physical sense, and although she knew most other lads around Covington would, she was thankful that he was different. Tonight he would get the reward for his patience: her heart and soul, and she would give it willingly.

Although the unthinkable lurked in a corner of her mind, she refused to heed it. It wouldn't be their only time, because Alex would come back to her and they would start afresh. For tonight they could pretend there was no war. No barrier to their eternal happiness. Several girls that she knew, who had gone to the same school growing up as her peers, had gone through many beaux in the years that she and Alex had been together, and some of those girls now waited each day for the postman with a sense of dread. The inky darkness had descended and she looked at Alex, noticing he had removed his shirt and that his braces hung down against his trousers. He smiled his most engaging boyish smile and it lifted her heart as he was still a boy; in some respects, while she through circumstances had been forced to mature more quickly. His widow's peak flopped down over his eyes as she came towards him, accepting his outstretched hand. She was convinced the boy to whom she gave herself tonight would come back to her, a man, hardened probably by his experiences which she knew were bound to change him. She had kept him safe with her, longer than many young women had, but despite having bowed to the inevitability of his leaving, for tonight he would be hers alone, and all that mattered in the world to them was each other. All her father had said when she told him of their plans was to trust her instincts, trust her heart, and that for tonight, all she needed to be, was happy.

Alex kissed her. 'I *love* you Laura Weston. I always will – and – I...'

Smiling, Laura put a finger to his mouth, before he could say another word. She placed his hand against her heart and he felt it beating faster. Within seconds, she was naked before him. He had watched her undress and then taking her face in his hands, he kissed her softly on the mouth. Her heart was lifted by his tenderness and as he lay on the bed, he held out his hand for her, nodding gently his encouragement, and she knew instinctively that he was giving her a last chance to pull back, to change her mind, before the dynamic in their relationship changed forever.

The look in her eyes told him she wanted this. So she knelt on the bed and within seconds, she was beneath him and the moment to consummate their love had come. His legs stroked her thigh and she convulsed beneath him, digging her fingers into the flesh of his back, trying not to gasp as she felt his first thrust, smiling as he soothed softly into her ear. Soon there was a rhythm to their lovemaking and she committed herself to it, as they made love at regular intervals throughout the night. After the last time, before sleep consumed them in the early hours, she pulled his arm around her shoulders, cushioning her head on his arm as his leg continued to stroke her thighs, his hand against her breast.

She smiled impishly in the darkness and said, 'You know what this means don't you?' Alex looked at her, with intent, shaking his head. 'We're bound together now, for eternity. Whatever happens.' Alex kissed the top of her head and then he succumbed to the sleep of a contented man.

Alex hadn't wanted Laura to see him leave the next morning, so he slipped quietly out of bed, dressing in the weak wintry February sunlight. He put on his khaki uniform for the first time, fastening the buttons with trembling fingers. He took his grandfather's watch and ran a thumb over it, and then he dropped it into the pocket of her coat. He had said he was leaving it with her for safe keeping and to remember him by, just as he always remembered his maternal-grandfather at moments such as this.

Out of a sense of duty and nothing more, he had informed his mother the previous evening that he was enlisting and all Effie could mutter in her gin-soaked self-pity was that it was about time he did his bit, for King and Country, before lamenting the end of her latest ill-conceived relationship. So he had left her to wallow, in her favourite seat in the saloon bar of the *Wheatsheaf Inn*.

Fully dressed, he looked down on the sleeping figure of Laura. The one person *still* worthy of his love. He kissed her forehead with tenderness to ensure she wouldn't wake, and gently he opened the door, looking back one last time to sear the image of her lying there to memory. He had written her a letter which he had left with George, because she had never wanted him to volunteer, consistently urging him to bide his time and wait for conscription.

'I love you Laura Weston!. *Always* remember that!'

Alex walked out without turning back, heading for the station where the other volunteers from the surrounding villages had been instructed to report. He went with a heavy heart, but he didn't believe it made him a coward, or any less a man to confront the reality of what he was doing, and to admit that now, when the time had come, the prospect of going to fight in France; scared the hell out of him.

★ ★ ★

When Laura woke and realised that she was alone in the large double bed above the *Covington Arms*, she shed large silent tears, because she understood *why* he had done it this way. Even so, she loved and hated him for it, all the same.

10

The second time Lavinia saw her husband in uniform, she gasped at just how handsome he looked, and in that moment, she was forced to acknowledge that despite everything she had come to learn about his motivation for courting her, and how *cunning* he must have been, she remembered *why* she had said yes, with *so* little hesitation.

Daniel stood in the drawing room of the townhouse, with its view of Cavendish Square. His mood was pensive as he accepted her perfunctory kiss on the cheek. She regretted having responded to his request to meet as if her acceptance was such hard work.

'You look good. Fighting fit!' She tried keeping her tone neutral and if he had taken her comment as sarcasm, he gave no indication. She had accepted it might possibly be the last time she would see her husband, and whatever else she felt now in light of what she saw as his deceit, she would never wish that. It would change the dynamic of everything as she was not as yet –despite all their efforts– with child.

'I only wished I felt ready,' Daniel said, his tone wistful. Since receiving his call-up papers, he had been in training, having joined the Hertfordshire Regiment with the rank Lieutenant, he had been informed there would be scope for promotion. He wasn't optimistic of impressing his senior officers, and his main concern was survival. He only wished he was confident of achieving that.

'You may surprise yourself. Do try to buck up Daniel or else you'll be a sitting duck. You're carrying the Swiffen family honour into battle remember!' Daniel pulled a face. 'Indeed. Since when has the Swiffen family honour mattered to you?'

Lavinia clutched her bag tighter under her arm, trying not to bristle with the simmering anger she felt. Would it be possible for her and Daniel, to ever have a civilised conversation again?

'Please don't let us part on a quarrel. I know you're apprehensive about military action, but I'm sure you are not alone in feeling that way. In the moment you may even surprise yourself. Life has never tested you has it Daniel; until now? You have this opportunity to *prove* yourself. For you to lead your men and for them to rely upon you. I am confident you won't disgrace yourself.'

Lavinia paused to glance at the clock. 'Is that the time? I was hoping to catch the train back to Hertfordshire. What time do you have to report?'

'Four o'clock. You don't have to go back to *Javrons* tonight. Stay here and we could have lunch?' She wanted to say yes, even felt *obliged* to, but still she hesitated and didn't succeed in covering. The marriage she had bore little resemblance to what she had expected, and she realised the extent to which she now blamed Daniel and her brother for that. Eavesdropping on their heated argument had been a mistake and it had changed everything, confirming her worse fears for Andrew, who she knew lacked self-control, but Daniel, who had consistently sought to underplay the strength of his friendship with Andrew, was equally *culpable*.

Finally she shook her head. 'I'm sorry, but I think it's better for us not to prolong the ordeal of saying goodbye. You'll be due leave in time and who knows the end of the war may not be too far ahead.'

Daniel cursed under his breath, banging a fist against the back of a chair. He approached Lavinia, holding both her arms in his hands, his grip tightening as he bent to kiss her on the mouth, until she pulled back, astonished. 'You want us to do that now? You want that to be the last memory I have of you prior to going off to fight?'

She put her hand to her mouth to stifle a gasp as she looked at Daniel, realising just how serious he was. 'Why not? I still have obligations to the Swiffen name. It is my duty to produce an heir, and as my wife, thus far, you have failed to abide by yours.'

'How dare you? My God I have tried!. Every time you deign to summon me to your suite to perform my "wifely" duties, I hope this will be *the* time; that I conceive, so at least we can both be spared the ordeal for awhile.'

For a moment Daniel couldn't bear to look at her, because he didn't want Lavinia to see his shame. Because she was right. When he sent word for her to come to him, he was usually *so* imbued with Cognac, that he could barely perform. Foreplay was dispensed with and lovemaking – if it could be described as such–was an *ordeal*. Another means to an end, that had come to encompass all their marriage was, because he didn't love her in the way that he should, and he probably never would.

Lavinia looked at him and he couldn't be sure if it was contempt or pity he saw in her eyes. Perhaps it was both, then turning she left the room. When the front door slammed he heard it reverberating throughout the cavernous emptiness of the house. He watched Lavinia, pausing on the front step, to take huge deep breaths. Although she felt ashamed to even think it after today and the confrontation they'd just had, if Daniel were to suffer the fate, he *so* feared, it might be the best outcome for them both.

France – Some weeks later

Daniel saw his first significant action in the trenches at Neuve Chapelle in the Artois region where his regiment were crucial in holding the Allied line. He suffered a flesh wound in the left shoulder, which he insisted was only minor,even though his friend Lieutenant Fearns badgered him to visit the CCS. He did write home regularly, describing in vivid detail the harsh realities of life at the Front, which he said, once experienced, was guaranteed to banish any lingering romantic notions of war. He also emphasised the point Lavinia had made, that when the time came for him to show his mettle as a soldier, he wouldn't be found wanting. When the Earl showed Lavinia this portion of the letter, she merely smiled, having kept the details of her last conversation with Daniel to herself. Although his letters to her were equally newsy, full of trivia, in which she held little interest, he told her —aside from apologising for his conduct on the day he reported for duty – little that was likely to offer much encouragement that relations between them would improve once his war was over. She felt increasingly lonely with nobody to confide in, and ashamed by the sham her marriage had become so quickly.

His accusation that she had failed to do her duty by him as a wife, had cut very deep, and an apology on the page lacked sincerity. She would struggle to forgive him those parting words as they confirmed that she was *only* a means to an end, and once she had given him what he required, there would be nothing left for her.

Covington, Devon – Spring, 1915

Laura Weston by contrast longed for the letters she received from Alex. She now awaited the arrival of the postman with the same level of excited anticipation; that once she had waited for him. Her green eyes dancing merrily each time, she was handed a letter, she knew had come from France. She had come to terms with why he had left her sleeping that morning, thus denying her the opportunity to say goodbye. She hadn't forgiven him, but she *understood*.

His letters were full of news and each made her miss him more; her days were long and empty without him. It was, she said, as bad as she had imagined it would be, after he had gone, and George, who saw her spirits visibly sag on the days when the postman didn't call, had no words with which to console her. To make matters worse, Charlie Stoughton saw Alex's departure as an opportunity and he had become emboldened in his pursuit of her. Her contempt for him acting as a spur, rather than to deter him. He would appear at the cottage door whenever George's back was turned, with his trademark lascivious grin, which suggested that no woman could possibly resist him, sufficiently conceited to believe that he could give any lass who caught his eye a good time.

The first time he shared that pearl of wisdom with Laura, she treated him to her usual sneer, but as he approached, she said. 'Take another step and I'll brand you with this for life.' She had reached for the iron warming on the fire and Stoughton hesitated. She never understood why he wasted so much time on her when she gave him no encouragement. She knew he liked a challenge, but he made her skin creep.

He laughed nervously. 'Your spirit is admirable, but I'll wear you down eventually. Just ask any of the Covington lasses who have had me in the sack. They'll tell you what you're missing.'

Laura sneered at him in disgust. Sadly, though he was right. She knew there were any number of local young lasses who had allowed loneliness to overcome them and had given into an oaf like Stoughton. She half turned away from him. 'You're a vulgar man and I can't imagine any lass, I would want to know having anything to do with you! But I guess there's some with no taste who might be so desperate. Now when I turn around I want to see you gone.'

Stoughton shrugged, treating her to his toothless grin, he put both hands on the doorframe, taking another step onto the threshold, until he and Laura,simultaneously heard the crack of a whip behind him and reeling, Stoughton shouted, 'What the hell?'

'I warned you that if I caught you sniffing around Laura I'd have you, but you wouldn't heed me, because you never do. You always have to push back. Well let that be a lesson to you. Laura's a cut above the kind of lasses you normally go after, the ones propping up the bar in the WheatSheaf most nights, so do yourself a favour, go after them, because my daughter is way out of your league.'

Stoughton put a ragged old handkerchief to his bleeding arm and said. 'A cut above is she? Well you could be right. Pity her boy's mother ain't so discerning. Shows what low-grade stock Conyer was dragged up from. I've seen poor Effie Conyer offering herself to anyone for a tot or two of gin!'

'Alex has the measure of his mother so your saloon bar tittle tattle has no value here, so get out of my sight Stoughton! Now!'

Stoughton pressed down on his congealing wound and left. Laura, folding bed sheets, gave her father a rueful look. 'You didn't have to step in like that Dad. I can *handle* Stoughton.'

'Yes, well he pushes his luck with me. I know you can stand your ground with him lass, but he's not averse to handling the female passengers when it suits. I'm just hoping that one day he'll push his luck with the wrong one and see himself come unstuck.'

'I guess the managers at Exeter would have to act then,' Laura said with more reassurance than she felt. George threw her a rueful look and left and she returned to her ironing, running the heavy object over the sheets with an increased urgency as she allowed her thoughts to linger on the vile Stoughton. She *did* have the measure of him, but she feared for her Dad. Being the station master at Covington meant everything to him and she wouldn't want him putting that at risk for her sake. They were both convinced that Stoughton had an ally or more where it mattered at Great Western, and she knew with a sense of dread that if Stoughton pushed her father too far, he could snap, with dire consequences for them both, as the roof over their heads depended upon him keeping his job.

France – Spring, 1915

From above they could hear sporadic enemy shelling, drowning out the shouts of their men, closer by. Daniel looked in the makeshift mirror, that Lieutenant Fearns was holding up, so that he could examine the wound to his left shoulder. He had been amazed to find his best man had been assigned to the same battalion, effectively as his second in command, although Martin's badgering him about returning to duty too quickly had become tedious; he knew it came from genuine concern, and having someone he trusted completely alongside him in the trenches was a boost.

'That seems to be healing up nicely.'

'You think?' Fearns asked, as Daniel smiled, throwing him a rueful look. 'How is Lavinia?' Fearns asked suddenly, throwing Daniel off kilter with his random question. How much should he confess about the trouble his marriage was in? Circumstances had forced his hand, and were it not for the bloody war, he couldn't imagine ever considering Andrew Restarick's sister as a viable candidate for his wife. When he looked in the mirror, to examine his conscience, he couldn't claim to do so with pride. It was scant consolation that he wasn't alone in his predicament. How many other sons of the estate had been forced to marry in haste? He still believed that he would have been happier with Olivia Trentham, until his ambitions there had been thwarted, and his friendship with Stephen, becoming a casualty of his ambition. He half turned fastening the buttons on his shirt with trembling fingers.

'Frustrated I think that she wasn't with child when I left. It's what we hoped for prior to my call-up, and I fear Restarick has been indiscreet in some of his discussions with her. I had always known they were especially close, but I still thought I could rely on him.' Daniel blushed slightly, as he felt a little guilty for blaming Andrew, as it felt too convenient.

'You should still get that shoulder looked at, the dressing changed, and I kind of promised we would look in one of our men admitted yesterday. Boost his morale.' Fearns looked at him encouragingly.

'I can tell that you are not going to let this go, so yes. Who are we seeing?'

'Private Earol Connor. Between you and me he's a mess, mentally speaking, and I doubt he should be passed fit to return, but you know what the hierarchy are like.'

Daniel nodded. 'Ok, but I hope *this* is an errand of mercy for Connor's sake, and not a ruse, because my shoulder is fine, Lieutenant.'

Martin Fearns smiled to himself as they left the dug-out and walked along the trench. The enemy fire was constant, but not too heavy, and soon they were in the staff car, making its short journey to the Casualty Clearing Station.

'So what's wrong with Connor?' asked Daniel, breaking the companionable silence. He didn't boost the men's morale anywhere as well as Martin so he left it to him.

'Physically I doubt there is much that will prevent him returning to the lines, but I think he's a liability. Whether the MO will be convinced I'm not sure, but if you see for yourself what he's like, your input can't be overlooked.'

Daniel shook his head, slowly. 'The MO's report will be strong enough for the Major. It's him we will have to convince.'

Fearns looked at him closely. 'What's wrong?'

'I fear I'm becoming immune to it all. The death, the wounding. The whole damn mess! An adequate coping mechanism I guess, but the day I got the call-up I was petrified. Scared that I would be done for in the first week of combat, and now look at me. Lavinia gave me quite a pep talk. Told me bluntly to buck up! Although I can't see that tactic working on Restarick when he's called up.'

'I always believed you would be mentally tougher than you'd give yourself credit for. You were superb in the offensive at Neuve Chapelle, and you've got the scars to show for it. I guess this war has given you the opportunity to prove something to yourself.'

Daniel looked at him sharply. Coming from Lavinia that would have sounded like a caustic barb and intended as such, but Martin was different. It forced Daniel to evaluate issues about himself that he had never before had to confront. He was considering his response when the car came to a halt. They alighted, with Daniel taking the lead, as they headed into the marquee of row upon row of makeshift beds and stretchers. They called to a passing orderly, 'Private Earol Connor?' who waved them in a general direction, so they walked briskly past countless beds in which young men, some of whom were barely old enough to have started shaving, looked on, exhausted with battle weary eyes, in this *unimaginable* hell. It made Daniel cross and there were occasions when he struggled to contain his anger, and not just for his own sake, but invariably for those under his command. They were kept here in this temporary hospital, a halfway house between the Front and a Field Hospital, which if they were lucky they would be transferred to, but for those with only superficial wounds, the CCS would offer only temporary respite before they were passed fit to return to action.

Daniel finally came to a halt at the foot of the bed which had been pointed out to them and hesitated when Fearns put a restraining hand on his arm. Turning abruptly to a nurse he said. 'We have been misdirected. I asked for Private Earol Connor, and one of your orderlies pointed us here. This man is not in our regiment, let alone our battalion.'

Daniel smiled at the young man in the bed. He had been wounded in the chest. 'What is your name?' The smile he received in return was equally genuine. 'Private Conyer, Sir. Devonshire Regiment.'

Daniel shook his hand warmly and they both felt a frisson of something. A connection which neither understood, but in that moment Daniel feared it might be attraction. He froze and Fearns looked at him quizzically. Alex Conyer removed his hand swiftly. He had also felt something and looked at Daniel strangely, as if he knew him, but couldn't remember where from.

'Nurse this is quite unacceptable. We came to see Private Connor of the Hertfordshire Regiment and because one of your orderlies didn't listen we have been brought to the bed of a Devonshire Regiment recruit.'

Daniel turned to Fearns smiling. 'It's ok. Errors occur sometimes. It's good to have met you, Private Conyer.'

The nurse looking embarrassed led them away to an adjoining marquee, filled with more beds with equally young soldiers. 'Lieutenant, I can only apologise that you were misdirected.'

Fearns smiled weakly and as they walked he looked at Daniel. 'What occurred back there with the Devonshire recruit?' Daniel shook his head. Turning he looked at Fearns, with pleated brows. 'You seemed surprised as if you knew him, that's all.'

'I guess he must have reminded me of someone. It's all

been rather an unfortunate misunderstanding. So let's speak to Connor, and get back to the Front.'

Fearns nodded hesitantly and Daniel hoped he had covered sufficiently, because he knew he had felt something when he had shaken the recruit's hand and the force of his reaction scared him.

As the two officers passed Alex Conyer had shuddered momentarily. An instinctive reaction to which Nurse Chagal responded swiftly. 'It's ok, those men meant you no harm, they were just angry they had been sent to the wrong patient.'

'It's not that,' Alex murmured and the French nurse stared at him curiously. She tucked in his sheets and ran her hand against his forehead. Her accented English was strangely alluring and he knew she was immensely popular with other patients. She was kind to him and a little flirty, which he was sure must be against the rules, but it had only a marginal effect on him, as his devotion to Laura was *unswerving*. He had, however, felt another reaction today with the officer, that was like nothing he had ever experienced before. It had been powerful and immediate and truth be told, he couldn't be sure he didn't want to experience it again.

'Rest now, they have gone.' She looked down at the pile of letters he had collected from home. Covington seemed a world away from the hell of the Front, but he longed for it now in a way he never would have before. So perhaps Laura was right about that as well. The ties of home bound you even when you *strived* to resist them.

'You're a popular man.'

'Laura likes to write a lot.'

'She is your girl?'

Alex blushed slightly, nodding. 'I'm a very lucky man.'

Nurse Chagal shook her head. 'She is the lucky one.' She reached for the creased photograph he kept of Laura with him, always.

'May I?' Alex nodded and she looked at it for a moment and wished she was Private Conyer's girl. She had been tending him long enough to know what kind of man he was. He might not be as classically handsome as Etienne de Valois, but he didn't portray her former lover's arrogance, that only seemed to stem – in her experience at least – from those who came from the privileged classes. Etienne had exuded it from every pore and she had come to resent him for it, but a man like this would not throw his girl off, on his mother's say so, of that she was sure. As she gave him the photograph back, her hand brushed across his, and she smiled. She had she knew, been accused of being over familiar, with some patients, but she had shrugged the criticism off, as the jealousy of her fellow nurses. She just wanted to feel as a vibrantly passionate, woman again as that wretched aristocrat had once made her feel, and perhaps a poor wounded English Private, who avidly guarded the worn photograph of his beloved girl could give her the affection she craved, the devotion that she felt was her due, and no petty regulations were going to deny her that.

The Trenches – Evening

Daniel sat in his dug-out, with Fearns opposite on the edge of his bed. Both were smoking, Daniel reflective, comfortable in the silence, although he suspected Martin blamed himself for the fiasco at the CCS.

'I am sorry for the mix-up. That Sister has a sharp tongue on her.'

Daniel, amused, nodded. He was glad to have Martin fighting alongside him and if only he could stop trying so hard to justify himself, and then apologising for coming up short, by his own exacting standards, Daniel knew his best man was way ahead of him in possessing the qualities required to make an officer.

114

'Forget it. You're right about Connor though. He's far from ready for a return to action. I can make my recommendations to the Major, now that I have seen him, which is what our trip to the CCS was all about?' He ignored the impish smile, adding, 'The man *is* an emotional wreck.'

Fearns nodded. 'That Private Conyer made quite an impression on you though. Have you never met him before? Maybe he was on the same troop ship coming out...'

'I said earlier, he must have reminded me of someone else. So I don't know why you're persisting with this. He was part of the mix-up. Nothing more,' Daniel snapped, and although he knew his reaction was irrational, he wasn't going to be probed by the best man at his wedding of all people.

He stood up, his back to Fearns, and stubbed out his cigarette. He shuffled some papers on his desk and without turning, he asked, 'Who's on patrol tonight?'

Fearns reeled off the names. It was so rare for Daniel to snap that he was shocked and knew better than to probe further.

'Tell one of them to stand down. I'm putting myself forward.'

'Yes sir.' Martin left to inform one of their battalion they were relieved of the night patrol. It was an avoidance tactic, but from what?

He had taken one last look at Daniel, prior to leaving. Daniel reaching for his cigarette case lit another one, and swearing under his breath, he banged his fist against the table. As covering tactics went, he had been hopeless. He needed to get a grip of himself. If it required him to do night patrol to achieve that, then so be it. There was nothing rational about his reaction to Martin's query, than there was to how he had felt when shaking Conyer's hand. He wouldn't allow himself to slip up again. Not here. There was no reason why he should ever set eyes on the Devonshire volunteer again and yet even that probability didn't satisfy him. So what would, damn it? Their encounter had been a one-off. A mischance, so why couldn't he just push it to the back of his mind? Worst of all why, when that was the most likely and expedient outcome, did it make him feel *so* wretched?

★ ★ ★

Eloise Chagal pulled the starched white cap from her head, letting her hair fall free, just as she heard the inebriated murmuring of her landlady, Helenê Duvalier. Grimacing as she had wanted to retire without being seen. Helenê Duvalier could be difficult at the best of times, but almost always in her cups on the cheap Cognac, that Eloise was certain would be the woman's ruin. That or her bitter twisted heart.

'Bonsoir,' Eloise said wearily, pulling off her shoes.

'So how was your shift? Have you saved all the brave young men so they can go out and fight again, before indulging themselves with our womenfolk, whose hearts they are determined to break?'

'Feeling sorry for yourself again Madame?'

'Huh. You make fun of me all the time. I open up my home to you, yet all you can do is mock me. I wish now that I never shared my sorrow with you, because now all you do is mock. Have you had your heart broken by a man? Some callous brute who promised you much and left. Have you suffered that pain as I have done?'

Eloise had never consciously confided about how Etienne had forced her from his life, so it was just the same rambling of a bitter middle-aged spinster, and she had heard the story so many times she had lost count.

'You haven't opened up your home, to me. I am a tenant. Paying over the odds for a tiny drab room. You can't even claim that you're doing this for the war and the glory of France!'

'Huh,' Helenê Duvalier sniffed, took another swig of Cognac from a hip flask and then another, until Eloise prised the flask from her vice-like grip. 'I guess all those brave wounded soldiers have been captivated by your charms and your beauty. Now they believe they are in love with you! That you will love them back. Each one will be deluded into thinking they are the *one* you will surrender your heart to. Don't!! Don't give them your heart! They're not worthy of your affection. They never are!'

'Merci, but I don't need your advice Madame. I follow my own path. I *always* have.'

Helenê Duvalier waved her finger at Eloise, her speech slurred as she tried to focus on the younger woman leaning against the door frame. She lunged at her to retrieve the hip flask, but Eloise was too quick. 'No. You have had enough. The Cognac makes you maudlin. Sleep is what you need.

'Your path will lead you to heartache and ruin. You mark my words…'

Eloise shook her head. She had heard it frequently from the older woman, who was usually heavily imbued with either absinthe or cheap Cognac at this hour. So she left her to drift into the stupor, that was her nightly ritual. She went to her own room. For as much as she might have agreed with her, she pitied Helenê Duvalier more. For the first time in months though, there was no room in her dreams for Etienne de Valois. His place was taken by a young British soldier who proudly showed the photograph of his girl.

For the time being he would remain *her* secret and she would guard the affection she had for him fiercely. If in the days and weeks to come, before he was sent back into the trenches, she had the opportunity to show Private Conyer how much she cared, she would seize it, as *he* could be the *one* to banish the images of Etienne from her mind forever. Devoted girlfriend at home or not, Eloise meant to have him.

117

11

Alex felt he was in a deep malaise, struggling to recover from the injury which had brought him to the CCS and for which he knew he had incurred the scepticism of the medical team who had voiced their concern that he might be malingering to avoid returning to the Front. Although the MO was reluctant to sign him fit for return, Alex knew his CO was determined to have him back in action, and had lavished praise upon him, dangling the offer to promote him to the rank of Lance-Corporal, if he could overcome the mental block, which the CO had been led to believe was delaying recovery. Alex, however, had other ideas about what was the root cause of his lethargy. With this in mind, he had bribed one of the orderlies to take him to see Private Connor, the recruit from the Hertfordshire Regiment that he had been mistaken for.

The visit hadn't been much of a success as there was no doubting Connor's fragile mental state. Alex had learnt some valuable facts about the background and heritage of Lieutenant Swiffen, but sadly little that explained the extraordinary reaction they had experienced on meeting each other.

'Per... perhaps you met him before the war,' Connor stammered nervously.

'I don't see how I could, having never left Devon until I went into training.'

Connor shrugged his shoulders. Alex looked at him, and was overcome by pity. The young man was evidently ill-equipped for action. He acknowledged that he had adjusted to the realities of combat better than he had expected, but he doubted there could a more profound example of a man ruined by his experience of war.

'I'm sorry I disturbed you.'

'No – it's ok. Most of the other patients, don't bother with me.'

Alex took several cigarettes from his pocket, handing them to Connor, placing one between the man's trembling lips and lighting. Connor just nodded his thanks, he found it easier that way. Alex thought he detected tears welling, but didn't dwell on it, and before one of the nursing staff noticed him he summoned an orderly to take him back to his own bed.

'Swiffen is a fine officer according to the men under his command, but why would you be so interested? You're with the Devonshire, aren't you?' Alex nodded that he was, and when the orderly returned him to his bed, it was Nurse Chagal who eyed him suspiciously.

'So where have you been? The MO came on his rounds and I had to cover for you. I don't like lying. Nor was he convinced.'

She smiled sheepishly as she helped him back into bed. Alex liked her, but he felt guilty for it, as he feared he could get to like her more than he should, which would be disloyal to Laura. Besides his reaction to the Honourable Lieutenant Swiffen, whose men seemed to liken to a saint, troubled him enough without also giving Nurse Chagal any encouragement.

Alex couldn't forget the night he and some of his comrades were granted their first leave. Many like him had claimed to have girlfriends at home, some even confessing to having a fiancé, but all that was forgotten, lost in an alcohol-fuelled haze when they fell happily into the arms of a local prostitute. Not him though. Despite intense goading and encouragement, he had resisted the temptation, so he would remain faithful to Laura, in the physical sense as he had in his mind, but provocation had been intense.

He didn't care what they thought of him for abstaining, but being able to look Laura in the eye the next time he saw her mattered more than a few hours of a forgettable amorous adventure. His recurring thoughts about Lieutenant Swiffen troubled him deeply, and although erring in his resolve with Nurse Chagal might be easier to comprehend, it would still be seen as being unfaithful. That she tempted him as no others had was also concerning because Nurse Chagal provoked in him, a reaction that no female aside from Laura Weston ever had.

The memory of that last night in Covington came readily to mind and it had returned to him the night he had lay smoking in bed watching Nurse Chagal, as she washed her hair at the end of a very demanding shift. The most mundane of tasks, and yet she had performed it with such sensual awareness that he had been aroused by her. There was a profound allure to Nurse Chagal that he felt she must be aware of and which she exploited to the fullest, but he suspected a diffidence also. A woman who guarded her privacy as fiercely as she would her precious possessions, and although she had to know that she was the focus of many a soldier's fantasy, whilst far from home, she would be careful not to get too close. For them not to know too much. She had suffered a heartbreak of that he was sure, but her job demanded she maintain the distance she craved. Her mystery was part of her *allure* and she would cultivate it, at her whim. Alex knew that he was just one of the many patients who came into and left her care, who were bound to be as captivated, as they were intrigued by Nurse Chagal.

His link to home was, however, still very strong and was expressed in the many letters he wrote and received. For him, it helped alleviate the boredom. He had written Laura that he had been injured but he had played down the severity of his wounds, and he was more worried about her. She said little about Stoughton, even though they had voiced concern that she would be continuously tormented by the head porter as soon as *he* was gone. Could Laura be underplaying her torment at Stoughton's hands to reassure him, as he was by limiting the extent of his injuries? It would be so typical of her. He was, he knew, becoming aware of the temptations that many soldiers struggled with on leave, and that regular leave was seen by the hierarchy as essential for maintaining morale and to keep men focused on winning the war. Thus his horizons were being opened up to a whole world beyond what he knew within the tiny confines of Covington, and the horrors of the trenches aside those horizons were testing his commitment and loyalty to Laura, and the basis on which he believed his life had been founded, as it had never been tested before.

The Trenches – Same Evening.

Daniel sat in his dug-out as the sound of shelling reverberated above him, and he struggled with the third draft of a letter home. He found writing to Lavinia increasing difficult, but he was keen to maintain the pretence to his family that theirs was a happy marriage. She would, regardless of his fate in this war, remain his wife and hopefully – soon to be confirmed – as the mother of his child, so he had to ensure that her position within the family was firmly established. He owed her that much at least.

He had been back to the CCS where the MO had confirmed that, in his opinion, Private Connor shouldn't be returned to action. The man was a wreck according to the MO and his attitude, to Daniel's mind, had been unduly harsh and unsympathetic. He suspected the MO had been aware of his attitude as he had said that 'weak' men like Connor shouldn't have volunteered for action, if they knew they weren't mentally equipped for it. Daniel had bitten his tongue at the temptation to say that he too had felt nervous on receiving his call-up papers. The MO lacked basic tact and was devoid of sensitivity, and although Daniel suspected he would rather be practising medicine anywhere but in this unimaginable hell, he had wanted to say that Connor would certainly prefer to have remained doing whatever he had before the war, but God only knew what he was fit for now as a result of the trauma he had endured.

He hadn't of course, but he realised now that he had been sorely tempted, if only to put that upstart of an MO in his place. Although he had gone to the CCS without Martin, he had struggled to resist the *urge* to visit the Devonshire recruit, Private Conyer. How could a simple mistaken identity have such a profound effect on him? He couldn't in all conscience have strayed into the wrong marquee and claimed a clerical error just to know if meeting Conyer provoked the same reaction in him without looking foolish, and he wasn't going to give that damned medic the satisfaction.

Determined to brush the image of Private Conyer from his mind, he looked down at the meagre four lines he had struggled with all evening. Most of what he had written was repetitive and mundane. He wouldn't blame Lavinia for throwing it straight onto the fire. He didn't dare imagine what kind of a marriage he would return to should he survive the war, if he was still being tormented by what Stephen Trentham had famously called his *"proclivities"*. The relationship would be doomed. Conyer had to come under that category, although he was damned if he would admit to an infatuation. He wasn't falling into that trap.

'Damn you Private Conyer! Why do you *insist* on intruding upon my thoughts? You have no place there.' He threw down his pen and grabbing at the sheet with the meagre few lines, he screwed it into a ball. What a bloody waste of time!

'Get a grip!' He said over and over as he paced the dug-out. 'Get a blasted grip!!'

He didn't dare to think if Conyer had given *him* a second thought since their all too brief encounter. Why should he when the problem was all in *his* head? Images of his time at Eton flashed through his mind and suddenly he saw an image of Private Conyer there, when it had no business being, supplanted into an environment in which he didn't belong by the sheer force of *his* imagination. If Stephen Trentham was here now, he would be shaking him into some sense, forcing him to get a hold of himself, and he would see Conyer as a threat to his reputation, but only because Daniel was keen to make him one which had so frequently been Stephen's main concern. How could he hope to function as an officer, to conduct his duties as such, and to fight the enemy on the other side of the trenches when the demons in his mind demanded he fight them first?

He sat down on his bed and fought the *urge* to shout out, above the sound of the shelling. He could feel beads of sweat forming on his forehead, because he had been here before, or at least he felt he had, because the demons he could feel tormenting him, now were the imagined ones, and the real flesh and blood ones, that Stephen had fought so vigorously to shield him from, were, he realised, the demons, he had been fighting against, for most his adult life.

★ ★ ★

Within days the MO was passing Alex fit to return to action, and although it was a decision he had expected, and it met the tacit approval of his CO who was concerned that Alex would return to the trenches the same committed volunteer he had been before his injury, but he agreed to three days leave. Alex was delighted, but felt it too long. Idleness never suited him and the many hours he had spent in bed at the CCS gave him too much time to think, his thoughts drifting in directions he hadn't wanted them to go. Having too much time to think wasn't doing him any good and so with the encouragement of several comrades who had also been granted leave, he had surrendered to their pleading and cajoling, to go into the nearest town and avail himself of its pleasures.

Eloise had been sorry to see him go. The attachment she had formed with him had been noticed, however, and she felt she was being watched, albeit slyly, by her fellow nurses; whether it was motivated by their spiteful jealousy or at the Sister's behest she wasn't sure. Sister Hopkins was she knew, still inclined to defend her, given just how adept she was at making patients feel better. Morale was an issue with some of the more severe casualties and she had a gift for boosting their confidence, but there was still a line that shouldn't be crossed and Sister Hopkins was consistently concerned that Nurse Chagal veered all too close to it, on numerous occasions. She still had a tendency to alienate her colleagues, but Sister Hopkins was shrewd enough to realise that it wasn't always her fault. Nurse Chagal was extremely attractive and that would *inspire* envy.

'I've been told that she's a loner. Too aloof,' the MO said bluntly.

Sister Hopkins inclined her head. 'Yes, she can be, but she's also a damned good nurse and we're not blessed with an abundance of them. I have seen for myself that she has a purely instinctive capacity for empathy with patients, and that can also inspire jealousy among her colleagues.'

'The men are only in her care for a limited time, Sister, before they are transferred to the Field Hospital or deemed fit for action. They're no good to their comrades if they've gone soft.'

Sister Hopkins nodded again, thoughtfully adding, 'You think this may have happened with Private Conyer?'

'It was borderline. Could have gone either way.'

She exhaled on a deep breath. For all her nursing qualities and talent for empathy, Nurse Chagal exasperated her. She found herself defending her more, than she did any other nurse in her charge and taking her file, she added the MO's comments, as she was compelled to do, leaving her to wonder if the French nurse's talent and her natural empathy was close to becoming a luxury that she could no longer afford to indulge.

★ ★ ★

Alex wasted no time enjoying his seventy-two hours leave, the longest he had enjoyed since arriving in France, his CO having granted it, in the hope it would sort him out and Alex shared the sentiment. Although he didn't believe that getting himself accustomed to the pleasures of the flesh provided by the local girls was necessarily the best tonic, the steady flow of wine and cheap Cognac saw him swiftly over the edge, until his mood turned maudlin and he confessed to missing Laura, terribly.

While several of his comrades claimed to have a sweetheart waiting at home, Alex wasn't as adept or as casual as they appeared to be at forgetting *them* in a fog of alcohol, and although they tried reassuring him that whatever liaison, he enjoyed tonight would mean nothing the next morning, and that the girls who wanted to have a good time with him knew it meant nothing, Alex couldn't be so cavalier. It didn't come naturally to him to deceive Laura, so casually, and when another volunteer reminded him mockingly that if his next twenty-four hours in the trenches proved to be his last, then being faithful will have counted for nothing, Alex's instinct was to fight him until another two Devonshire volunteers intervened. 'We should get him into a billet for the night before he challenges the entire regiment to a fight.'

There was humour in his voice as he wrapped Alex's arm around his shoulder, leaving his comrade to take Alex's other arm as they led him out of the bar, one of them grumbling about young volunteers who couldn't hold their liquor.

They reached the cobbled central square, when a young woman stopped them. 'Where are you taking him?'

'To find him a bed. We warned him to pace himself, but he ignored our advice. He was in some hurry to get drunk, and now he's become *our* problem.'

'Very considerate of you to show so much concern for one of your men. Leave him to me. I'm a volunteer nurse at the CCS. This man was in my care until only midday, when the MO signed him fit for action. He doesn't look fit for anything now.'

One of the soldiers had no hesitation in abandoning his responsibility, the other was more sceptical. 'You're sure miss?'

'Oui! I rent a room over there.' She pointed at her landlady's house. 'If you could bring him, I shall make it worthwhile.'

'La...ura?' Alex slurred the name, recognising the female voice on a subliminal level.

'He's all yours cherí, as much good he'll do you tonight.'

'I told you I am a nurse. Now once you have left him at my door, you can chase after your whore! Go! You can leave Private Conyer to me. I'll take care of him.'

The two soldiers looked at her quizzically, suspecting at last, that she probably was a nurse. She had to practically hold him up as she searched for her key and then she nudged him inside. She hadn't thought about how she was going to get him past Helenê Duvalier as yet, but was reassured that the old woman would already be drunk on Cognac. Part of her wondered why she thought this was a good idea, but she freely admitted to *lusting* after Alex Conyer, and she was convinced when it was offered to him, even in his cups, he would barely give his beloved Laura a second thought. *Hypocrite!* She shared some of her landlady's prejudiced view of men, well most of the men in her limited experience. Etienne, for all his education and breeding, was too weak to stand upto his mother. That was why she could only ever have been *his* mistress. He would have happily continued enjoying her pleasures if he could have, but she'd had too much self-respect to have become his *guilty* pleasure, kept in a dingy apartment on the Left Bank, a world away from the mansions of the 16th arrondissement, and the châteaux of the Loire. The war had been a great social leveller in some respects, and she could still relish the prospect of treating a wounded soldier of Etienne's class, to have their fate in her hands. For tonight, however, she would content herself with her English volunteer, whom fate had thrown into her lap. If in the morning, he struggled to confront the reality of his betrayal, of having been unfaithful to *his* beloved Laura, it would be futile for him to look to her for sympathy. He would be welcome to his guilt and he would only have himself to blame.

She urged Alex along the narrow hallway to a salon where he collapsed onto a chaise lounge, breathing heavily. Madame Duvalier appeared and seeing him she snorted derisorily 'What is he doing here?'

Her speech was slurred, and Eloise smiled. 'He's as drunk as you and he needs a bed for the night. So he will share mine,' she said it in a matter-of-fact tone which brook no argument, and Madame Duvalier was affronted.

'You think I run a brothel now?'

'Hush your mouth. You have been goading me into exposing his hypocrisy–as you call it–ever since I mentioned how attracted I am to him, the reaction he has provoked. Now you're going all moral on me. You have no need to worry. In the morning he'll wake in my bed and realise what he has done and I will have proved *my* point.'

'At the expense of my reputation in this town? Look at him! You think he's upto fulfilling whatever plans you have?' Eloise smiled. If the old hag was seriously worried about her reputation she had left it too late. 'Leave that to me. If he can't satisfy me sexually, no matter. It's what he will think we have done that will count. That will leave him writhen with guilt.'

Eloise smiled conspiratorially at Madame Duvalier, who, shaking her head, turned to leave. 'So what makes him so special? They are all hypocrites in their ways.'

'Listen to you. One bad experience with a lover and you've been at war with all men ever since.'

'I was jilted!' Madame Duvalier said the words with such vehemence that she left Eloise in no doubt that even after more than two decades the pain was still raw. Shaking her head, she shuffled away.

'Oui. That was cruel, but in a manner of speaking I was also jilted,' Eloise said to herself as she stood, her gaze fixed on Madame Duvalier's retreating back.

Eloise got Alex up to her room a while later, with the grudging assistance of her landlady, who stood leaning against the doorframe. The bottle of Cognac in her hand, she took a large gulp and snorted. 'You will have to undress him. For your plan to be authentic he will have to wake naked in your bed. Better still in your arms. Then there can be no doubt that he'll have betrayed his sweetheart.'

Eloise smiled. She hadn't planned to take matters that far, but Madame Duvalier was correct. It had to look convincing in the light of day. She would have to accept the probability that he would want nothing to do with her in the morning, or ever again, but he had to believe in his sense of shame, that in his loneliest moment he had *succumbed* to her and then the sense of betrayal would be complete.

★ ★ ★

Tiny fingers of light filtered through the black drapes as dawn broke the next morning. Alex woke slowly, with a sense of hesitation and in confusion as reality hit, that he was in a stranger's bed in an unfamiliar house and he had no idea how he got there. He turned. There was still the indent of another's head on the pillow beside him, and within a moment he was back in the ward at the CCS and the familiar face of a nurse was leaning over him. It was, he realised, Nurse Chagal, but what was she doing here? Unless it was him that didn't belong. Erotic images of Nurse Chagal swamped his mind and he couldn't push them out. Was it purely male lust that made him think of her now or were tangible memories of what had taken place last night forming in his mind? He had admitted being infatuated by her after he had witnessed the erotic scene of her hair washing at the CCS but surely that was all it had been? An infatuation. He knew he had been signed fit for duty, so there was no reason for him to be in her company now. He'd had his excess of alcohol last night and he had been maudlin, thinking too much of how he missed Laura, when he should have been enjoying his weekend leave as his comrades had been determined to do.

Nurse Chagal was too real to still be a dream. He could see her sensual lips, the evocative sway of her hips as she moved, and it was in his mind, but he could feel her presence also and that was driving him mad with delirium. He must have succumbed to her charms, there was no other answer. 'You've slept well.' she said casually leaning over him, and he realised now that his dream and reality had coalesced into one.

'I had enough to drink,' he stated, his Devonshire burr, more pronounced, as it usually was in moments of stress.

'Not so drunk that you couldn't perform your manly duties,' she nodded, adding, 'here in my bed.'

'We did it?'

'Made love? Oui! Magnificently so.' Eloise spoke in a very provocative French accent, smiling as Alex groaned inwardly.

'It is ok. Nobody needs to know, unless you want them to. I understand how some men like to boast of their prowess.' She bent to pull on the flat shoes in which she moved around the CCS, weaving between the beds, working her magic.

'You're sure we had sex?'

'Whichever way you choose to describe it, the answer is still yes. I prefer to say that we made love, but I understand there maybe guilt on your part.' Alex leaned forward as Eloise moved sensually around her bedroom, dabbing behind her ears with cologne.

'There's no maybe. I am in love with Laura. I *am* committed to her. She is the *only* girl, I will make love with.' Eloise stopped in the act of brushing her hair and smiled at him.

'Well on the evidence of last night's performance, that isn't true.' She shrugged and continued brushing. 'It does not matter, because we enjoyed ourselves, and it doesn't have to happen again…unless.'

Alex leapt out of bed and suddenly conscious of his nakedness he reached for his khaki trousers, pulling them on. Despite the banging in his head, he reached for Eloise, holding her firmly by the shoulders. 'This was never meant to happen and I assure you it will *never* happen again.'

Eloise shrugged, unperturbed by his earnestness. 'As you wish. Until the next time of course that you are in your cups and you feel the need for company. If so call me.'

'Is this just a game to you? Can't you even see what you have done? You have ruined everything!'

Eloise lifted the hand, holding the brush, brandishing it at him, and for a second he thought she was sufficiently angry to strike him with it, but her hand fell and the brush went to the floor.

She shook her head, very slowly and deliberately. 'I've

ruined nothing! Non, it is you that have ruined it for yourself. It's your guilt that is eating at you! You have binded yourself to this girl and the rules you have chosen to abide by. Unrealistic rules. I am attracted to you! I have been since you were first admitted and yes, maybe I did exploit the situation, last night. Your comrades were happily going to abandon you in the town square until I intervened. Yes, it's because I wanted us to make love, and this morning I have no regrets. So if you must repent, do it alone.'

Eloise moved to the door, opened it ajar and looked back at Alex. 'When you leave, please do so quietly and discreetly. My landlady is not disapproving, but she too is in her cups most nights, and she isn't at her best in the mornings. You do not want to incur her *wrath*!'

Alex reached out to grab her arm, and for a moment he wanted to hurt her physically by tightening his grip, but her warning look deterred him.

'I was so wrong about you. In the CCS you were *the* nurse all the patients wanted to have looking after them. Caring, gentle, but it's all an illusion. You're cold, cruel.'

His words cut deep, but she was damned if she would let him know how much, because she *cared* for him. 'What did you expect? Didn't they tell you about the realities of war Alex before shipping you out here to fight? To this unimaginable hell of the trenches and No Man's Land. It's survival of the fittest. Every man for himself first, then for his comrades, and if you're one of the lucky ones you may get to go home when it's all over and plead with Laura to forgive you, but go on as you are and you're doomed!'

Eloise left. Leaning against the door, she took a deep breath, willing the tears stinging her eyes not to come. She felt as if her legs would give way beneath her. She was hurting and she had said all that because she was, but she knew that she had said too much. In Alex she had at least seen some remorse, for what they had done. In Etienne de Valois, she had seen only arrogant self-righteousness as he had cast her from his life, but her reaction to these two men was bizarrely similar. Because they had forced her to see the folly of giving her heart too readily, and she reiterated now as she had then that no man would ever get close enough to use and *discard* her again.

12

London—June, 1915

Intense summer sun streamed through the window of the master suite at the Swiffen town house on Cavendish Square forcing Daniel to shield his eyes, from its glare as he tried to fasten the buttons on his shirt with trembling fingers. There was an uneasy silence in the room. The atmosphere tense between him and Lavinia as was so often the case these days. This had been his first prolonged leave since call-up, and had been brought about after the intense fighting his battalion had endured at Festubert in French Flanders, during which his best man, Lieutenant Fearns, had been seriously injured when in a rare lapse of judgement, he had gone over the top and into a hail of enemy shelling and was according to every medical assessment he had been subjected to, lucky to still be alive. Now Daniel was turning his attention to the ever-pressing issue of his ongoing failure to sire an heir. They only had sex now; there was no pretence of lovemaking between them. Each encounter was excruciating in its way as Lavinia did her duty by him and no more, and when she had accepted his invitation to meet in London, she had done so with a determination to lay her cards on the table and to *assert* her demands for the future terms of their marriage. She knew that divorce was untenable. He would never agree to it, nor was it a divorce she was seeking but an acceptance from him that she should live her own life, while heeding her responsibilities to the future Viscount Swiffen.

She sat now at her dressing table, with her back to him, slowly and methodically forcing the brush through her hair. When finally she spoke, it was barely above a whisper. 'Well that was painful.'

'Did I hurt you?' asked Daniel, concern pleating his brow as she turned slightly, realising from his tone, that it was genuine.

'I don't mean physically. How many more times *must* we put ourselves through this torture before reaping the benefits?'

'Conjugal relations aren't meant to be torture, nor do most couples view them as such, ' he said pointedly, making no attempt to hide his exasperation. He knew Lavinia readily laid the blame for their loveless sexual encounters at him, but he wasn't having it. She came to his bed in a frame of mind that was set to *endure* sex in a cold perfunctory manner all the joy sucked out and was then surprised by the outcome. He wasn't taking the blame for that.

Lavinia turned to face him and there was a blank expression on her face. She wasn't going to get over emotional. She didn't think he deserved her tears, so she wasn't going to shed them in front of him.

'Andrew said he tried to warn me against rushing into marriage. He saw that I was dazzled by your title and the trappings that came with it. It's a pity he couldn't have been as honest about his own feelings. Perhaps it's Stephen Trentham's advice I should have sought. For what it is worth your mother is *right*. Elizabeth says a baby will be a focus for my attention and maybe then I'll have done my duty and this ordeal that you subject us to will have been worth it, in a tangible sense anyway. I am intrigued though Daniel, had it not been for this wretched war, how much longer would you have put off the reality of marriage and *your* obligations to the estate?'

He signed heavily. 'I don't know!' he exclaimed in a weary tone as he sunk to the edge of the bed, reaching for her hand.

She pulled away and turning, she continued brushing her hair, caught by mid-afternoon sunlight. 'Are you staying in London tonight?'

'Yes, I am dining with Andrew. There's no need to ask, though, I shall succumb to this ordeal again, in case it hasn't worked this time.'

Daniel rose, shaking his head, he laughed mirthlessly. 'Thankyou Lavinia for adhering to your vows. I shall leave you in peace.'

'Are you going out?' she asked as he reached the door.

'I received a telegram from Stephen Trentham. It appears he wants to salvage our friendship, before it's too late. I could ask him for his opinion on whether I was being unfair to you by asking for your hand, although I suspect he's just relieved it wasn't Olivia who said yes.'

'How dare you be so flippant given what I have sacrificed to be your wife?'

'There wouldn't be a problem if Andrew hadn't unburdened himself on our wedding night. Your brother just never accepted the situation. Never managed to realise the consequences of acting on what he claimed to have felt, which would have led to the ruin of both our families.'

Lavinia slammed the brush down and, half rising, she contemplated coming at Daniel like a half-crazed shrew, but seeing her reflection in the dressing-table mirror, she slumped back down, hearing the click of the door as he left.

She forced herself to acknowledge, on that point, Daniel was right. She had been quick in accepting that Andrew had his *proclivities* and that she had been his confidante, his emotional crutch throughout his adolescence.

Stephen Trentham might well have advised her against marrying Daniel, had she known him well enough to seek his advice, but he might also have told her some home truths about her beloved Andrew that she wouldn't have found so easy to accept.

★ ★ ★

Several hours later, Daniel and Stephen Trentham sat opposite each other at their club on Northumberland Avenue. They had neither spoken nor corresponded in months, and Daniel had feared they might never connect again. The atmosphere was understandably tense. 'How is Lavinia?'

Daniel, pursing his lips, shook his head slowly to indicate his marriage was not the best topic of conversation.

'I had a meeting with Austin Westmacott about the forthcoming second volume of poetry, and he informed me that Olivia has joined the Voluntary Aid Detachment.'

Stephen nodded. He was immensely proud of his cousin, but he, like her father Edgar, found her stubborn streak exasperating.

'I think Edgar and myself are still waiting on her pardon. Her wrath is invariably spared but once unleashed it can be stinging.'

'I'm sorry!'

'For what? Stephen took a cigarette from his case and offering the case to Daniel, he lit his.

'Everything. Not urging you to attend my wedding. For putting you in an impossible position with Edgar and Olivia. Most of all for allowing our friendship to drift.'

'I think we have both been at fault in that regard. So how is life at the Front?'

'Hell. My Lieutenant and best man, you would remember Fearns? He took a hit at Festubert. He's lucky to be alive and *his* war is over. The future uncertain. So, you haven't been compelled to enlist?'

'I tried. I was told to bide my time. Conscription becomes ever more likely the longer the war continues and I was told my role at the Foreign Office was still of value. I am sceptical though, and there's no pride to be had in sticking to a desk job when so many of my peers are doing their bit. It doesn't look good, still being in civvies.'

'You should be grateful.'

Daniel always feared the reality of fighting and although he had performed better than he had ever imagined, surpassing the expectations of many, especially his father, he saw it as surviving, nothing more, and the horrors he had witnessed had him waking up in a cold sweat most nights. He guessed that if he were lucky to survive, then some of the images he would take from the Front would stay with him for years. Fearns' loss would also be keenly felt, as he knew he had relied heavily upon his Lieutenant's shoulders. On arrival at Victoria he had seen the invalid and dejected looking soldier, forlornly selling matches outside, his empty right sleeve pinned to his chest and Daniel recalled how grateful the soldier had been that an officer on leave stopped for a few moments, bought some matches and took the time to chat. As he turned to leave, Daniel had seen he was close to tears. A proud young man in his prime reduced to a tearful wreck, with a trembling lower lip. A husk of what he had once been, before this wretched war. He had walked away shaking his head and tried that night to obliterate the image of the soldier, just as he had to airbrush the image of Lieutenant Fearns falling backwards into the trench, as the shelling erupted around them, and being unable to help his friend while the heat of battle raged around them. Suddenly he was in the battle again, reliving it in his mind until Stephen's voice brought him back. He felt Stephen's hand brush his knee and he laughed.

'Careful you'll give the other patrons the wrong idea, which would be quite ironic given the times you were my main protector at Eton.'

Stephen laughed too. 'What I wouldn't give to go back to those days now.'

Daniel smiled wistfully. 'So how is Lavinia spending her evening?'

'Dining with her brother. Her ever faithful counsel of hope. She still doesn't accept that his indiscretion in speaking out on our wedding night is the root cause of our problems.'

Stephen suppressed a smile, drawing heavily on his cigarette, but it wasn't lost on Daniel.

'It's ok. You're entitled to be relieved. You were right to warn me against pursuing Olivia, even if she hasn't forgiven you.'

Stephen stubbed out his cigarette, taking a moment to study Daniel's troubled expression. For him tonight was about reconciliation. To re-establish the most enduring friendship he had ever known. Because reproach was a waste of time, compared with the waste being waged on a daily basis in France and Belgium. He was acutely aware of the possibility that he may be robbed of the chance of seeing Daniel again and who knew what his fate might yet be, before this wretched war was over.

'Let's eat.'

★ ★ ★

Later that evening Daniel nursed a Cognac between his hands in the library at Cavendish Square. Lavinia found him sitting in the dark. She switched on a standard lamp beside the fireplace flooding the room with light.

'How was your evening?' he asked.

'Fine. Yours?'

He nodded. 'It was good to catch up. So how is Andrew?'

'Scared. He's convinced himself that his time to be called is imminent and he's not handling it well. Father is urging him to volunteer and be seen to do the 'right thing.' He also fears he will be targeted by the other men, singled out – because, well you know why.'

Daniel suppressed a smile. He doubted Andrew Restarick would be able to control his urges, his instinct for impetuosity and woeful lack of discretion.

'I fear that once your brother comes to face the reality of the trenches, that will be the least of his concerns, providing he keeps his own counsel. He is right to be scared though, I would be scared for him because I doubt he is equipped to cope with life at the Front.'

'You have coped. Surprising yourself truth be told. Andrew might do likewise. He sends his regards by the way.'

Daniel smiled to himself, staring into the depths of his brandy snifter. 'Lavinia?'

She looked at him sharply. 'I'm tired Daniel, so I'm going up. I expect you won't be long.'

He reached out and took her hand, despite her resistance. He held it tight. 'I want us to make love tonight. Not to just go through the motions of having sex for the sake of it. The means to an end.'

Lavinia smiled. 'Isn't that precisely what our marriage has become?'

'Only if we allow it to continue. I'm saying let's try. I have been unfair to you, I accept that. You would call it deceit, but I never concealed why I had to marry, to produce a legitimate heir. You know that was my *imperative* from the start. In less than forty-eight hours my leave will be over. I'll be going back to the Front, for God only knows how long, to endure whatever fate has in store for me. Which may or not mean survival.'

He sighed heavily, looking at her and tightening his grip on her hand, adding. 'I don't want us to part like this.' Lavinia smiled, running her hand through Daniel's hair, moving closer so that their bodies meshed. She had to try, because he was

139

right. She could become a mother and a widow all at once, and what memories would she have of their child's conception, if she didn't acknowledge that Daniel felt a deep and abiding affection for her, even if it wasn't the love she had imagined their marriage would flourish under? She had been made aware of the importance of the Swiffen line of succession from the start. Her mother-in-law had reiterated it, more times than she cared to remember, since Daniel had been called to arms.

He looked up at her and she saw the plea in his eyes. She nodded soundlessly, biting her bottom lip. In the long term she doubted it would change very much between them, but for tonight she could experience the passion she had always hoped would be infused into her marriage and if this was to be the *last* time, she would have that memory and hopefully the resulting heir to show for her efforts.

At this moment, that had to be better than the cold emotionless sex, that she had forced herself to *endure* that afternoon.

13

France – 1916

Daniel had learnt to live without having, Martin Fearns alongside him in the trenches but it had proved a difficult adjustment. He hadn't realised the extent to which he had come to rely on Fearns and this along with the trauma of witnessing the extent of his injuries as he had fallen back into the trenches, had resulted in Daniel having numerous flashbacks which assailed him at intervals throughout the day, and dogged his attempts at getting a good night's sleep.

A promotion to the rank of Captain failed to bring him much solace, while his second-in-command, offered little support by way of boosting morale to either him or the men serving under them.

The Somme offensive which began on July 1st resulted in heavy losses from the start, further demoralising the troops. Survival had become a lottery and the sense that each twenty-four hours was being lived like it would be your last, became ever more acute. Daniel felt the burden weighing on him heavily. He had frequently looked to Fearns for a boost in his confidence before he attempted to rally the troops, sadly Lieutenant Sallis failed to provide him with that belief. Sallis wasn't an optimist. He took Daniel's orders like an automaton, believing in his gut that they were doomed. Given the losses suffered on the first day, Daniel found little reason to cast doubt on Lieutenant Sallis's grim prediction about the progress of the war.

Nationwide conscription introduced in March meant that any man aged between eighteen and forty-one could be called to arms, so the ranks were swelled by the new recruits, only to be immediately decimated by heavy losses. His own sense of doom appeared to have reduced as he realised, he had now survived eighteen months at the Front. He was corresponding regularly with Lavinia and while he wouldn't say that their exchange of letters was companionable, they had reached an understanding and he no longer saw writing to her, as such a chore.

Andrew's enlistment coming shortly before the Conscription Bill passed through Parliament meant Lavinia now had two men whose fate she worried about, while their latest attempt to sire an heir had, proved futile. Sat in his dug-out, he could hear the shelling above him. He should go out and be with his men, set a good example, but Lieutenant Sallis would doubtless see his presence as some kind of intrusion.

In the weeks since the Somme offensive began he had seen morale among his battalion diminishing rapidly. The growing toll of lost comrades and the sense that ground so hard won and at such huge cost was then lost to the enemy within days, if not hours, was sapping the mood of men who had endured almost two years of fighting, in a war that many had optimistically predicted would be over by that first Christmas.

The higher-ranking echelons were struggling to retain morale and he knew from reports at home that public satisfaction with the Government's conduct of the war was haemorrhaging, while faith that ultimately victory could be secured was ebbing away.

Taking his helmet, he went out into the trench as another shell hit. He heard Lieutenant Sallis issuing orders in his customary monochrome tone. He was flat, insipid; as unlikely to inspire confidence as the man relaying the railway timetable at Victoria Station. Sallis wouldn't have inspired him over the top, so he wouldn't expect the men to have any enthusiasm, for following the man either. Daniel knew he should rebuke him, but realised that despite his rank, he lacked the confidence to do so, wondering whether ultimately it would be counter-productive, and he suspected he was also letting the men down in that respect.

'Lieutenant how's it going?'

'Pardon Sir?' Sallis bellowed at him over the sound of the shelling.

'The men are obeying as you bid them?'

'Of course Sir!' he exclaimed, only just remembering to salute. Daniel could see he was affronted by the question, but he didn't care.

'It doesn't look like it to me.' Daniel pushed his way to the front of the trench blowing hard on his whistle. If the night was going to see a major offensive along this line, involving *his* men, he was damned if he would stand by and watch them perish for a woeful lack of leadership.

Having Lieutenant Sallis assigned to him maybe seen as a *fait accompli,* but he outranked him and Daniel was determined to show him what leadership was, damnit!

He called to his Corporal and they began discussing tactics, in hushed tones, as neither had much confidence in Sallis, and his doom-laden orders. He had heard the men bemoaning the absence of Fearns, who they had trusted as he had trusted him.

Martin Fearns' instinctive courage had invariably left him feeling ashamed, which he had readily acknowledged, but now Daniel realised the time had come for him to step up and demonstrate to his men the leadership they were seeking, and which his rank demanded, even if hitherto he had doubts that he was capable. They stood at the parapet of the trench, with rifles poised, their bayonets attached.

Daniel took his revolver from its holster, nodding gently at his Corporal. Lieutenant Sallis, ignoring him, turned away looking down at his feet. He wanted no part of what he considered an ill-advised sortie, but Daniel suspected this was his Lieutenant's view of most offensives they had engaged in. What did the man expect them to do? Hide in the trenches and dug-outs waiting for the enemy to come at them over the top. The Germans had suffered many setbacks, but they had also been resilient at regaining ground, hard won by the British.

It led Daniel to wonder if every battalion had their own version of Lieutenant Sallis, whose demeanour and conduct hampered progress. He'd had enough. He was going to show his *mettle* and let his men follow his example. Letting his fate fall as it may. He owed Martin Fearns some acknowledgement for the sacrifice he had made, the consequences of which his friend would live with for the rest of his life.

★ ★ ★

Eloise Chagal hadn't enjoyed the luxury of time in which to dwell too much on the consequences of the night, she had enjoyed having Alex in her bed. Nor had there been a second encounter, as she had hoped. In fact, as the weeks had passed, she had worried for a while, that he might have reported her and she wouldn't have wanted to rely upon Madame Duvalier's discretion such as it was. Her landlady was slowly descending into a Cognac-fuelled haze from which she might never emerge. It was an oblivion into which she readily succumbed to, each night and in Eloise's eyes she had become a figure worthy only of other people's contempt as the old woman had gone beyond pity.

The men in her care, however, relied upon her nursing

skills more than ever as the fighting in the Somme offensive intensified and each shift left her feeling drained, both physically and emotionally. She dreaded each time a new casualty was brought in, that it might be Alex Conyer, because despite all the resentment he now felt for her, and in reaction the anguished contempt she had heaped upon him the morning after, she realised, that however futile it might be, she had fallen for him. Hard. To the extent that she barely ever thought about Etienne de Valois now.

She had no idea about the fate of her former lover, but she didn't feel the same dread that she had once felt, each time a new admittance was brought into the marquee; that it might be the man to whom she had given her heart. He had, she knew, replaced Etienne in that respect, even though she may be doomed to lose in love *again*. The words he had said to her that morning had cut deep, but they altered nothing about how *she* felt.

Sister Hopkins had continued lavishing praise upon her when it was due, but also feared that at any time Nurse Chagal's secondment would cease, and she would be instructed to return to the Field Hospital at Etaples. Where once Eloise had no care for where she was deployed, now she *longed* to be close to Alex, to know he was surviving each offensive and if he were brought into the CCS again she would have the opportunity to care for him.

Sister Hopkins also found it frustrating how casually Nurse Chagal took praise with a nonchalant shrug. She wasn't inclined to give her praise freely, but she had seen for herself numerous occasions when in Nurse Chagal's case it was well earned, and she believed it should be accepted with good grace.

'It is impossible to remain detached from all this Sister. We fix these boys, and men up, and send them out to suffer the same or perhaps worse. How can anyone remain *immune?* Untouched by that?'

'You have to try, because the horrible unpalatable reality is that if you let it drag you down you'll be no use to anyone.

'You're doing a remarkable job Nurse Chagal…' she held up her hand to quell any protest, '… I have also come to realise that you're not one to let praise go to your head, quite the reverse in fact, so I have no hesitation in giving it. I acknowledge I had my doubts about you when you were first seconded to me – not about your abilities – your temperament, so please don't let me down now.'

'Merci.' With a slight nod she took her leave. There had been numerous shifts when her temperament had been severely tested and she found herself questioning her resolve. She could easily have finished many a shift by vowing she wouldn't return, but she had *endured*. Where she had found the inner core from sometimes she had no idea, but if Alex were to be brought in and he needed *her*, then she wanted to be the one tending his wounds, perhaps even help to save his life. Whether that was the mark of her as a good nurse or that she was compelled by the force of her love she had no idea, but it was her fate and there was no turning from it.

★ ★ ★

The intense fighting continued for weeks. Summer slid into autumn and with it came the rain, but no sign that the enemy's resolve was weakening. Losses were heavy and the toll on morale was like a dead weight. Daniel felt there had been no other time since arriving in France, that he would have benefited from having a second-in-command on whom he could rely. Sadly, Lieutenant Sallis was seriously lacking in this regard and Daniel was aware that the relationship between them had deteriorated as the weeks had gone by. He couldn't accuse Sallis of neglecting his duties, but knew he couldn't trust him either, while his Corporal had been to see him on two occasions, to voice the men's concerns about the Lieutenant. Sallis didn't give much of himself, so it was hard to gauge what he was thinking, about both the progress of the war and the strategy being adopted by the high command, for whom he had nothing but contempt. Sallis spoke a lot about class, which made Daniel feel uneasy, although he knew he wasn't the only target. Sallis was equally dismissive of Asquith and Lloyd George, whose motives he cynically questioned for committing Britain to war. Daniel found himself biting his tongue more than at any time he could recall, even when in receipt of his father's censure.

He was not inclined to make an enemy of Sallis, but he had drawn an invisible line, which the Lieutenant dare not cross without feeling, in full force, the consequences of his insubordination.

For himself Daniel would have benefited from a decent night's sleep. It wasn't just the shelling or the night patrols, that he volunteered for, it was the nightmare flashbacks that tormented him. Always the same image of Martin Fearns going over the top into a hail of enemy shelling, before falling backwards onto him. It was an image which haunted him more than any other that he had witnessed in this hell ever had.

Corporal Broom was a decent chap. Daniel could talk easily to him, recalling memories of Lieutenant Fearns, for whom they shared a mutual respect, just as many of the privates had. Sallis, however, was seen, Broom confided, as increasingly setting himself apart from the men, he was in command of and although not surprised to hear this Daniel was still alarmed. Given his politics, he understood why Sallis bore a natural antipathy to him, coming from the privileged class, but their volunteers came from all backgrounds, and Sallis had made no secret that although he considered himself a working-class man, it didn't prevent him adopting a condescending attitude towards those under him, whose optimism about the outcome of the war, and their faith in high command, he relished mocking.

There had also more disturbingly been reports that Sallis had no hesitation about telling some of the youngest and most vulnerable volunteers that their optimism was wasted. They were all going to hell and that the generals couldn't give a damn. This revelation was worse than any he had heard, and he thought about intervening, but erred on the side of caution. Having a gloomier outlook was hardly a crime. He decided he would keep his powder dry and bide his time, but he had the measure of Lieutenant Sallis and hoped that if he gave the man enough rope, he would be hung by his own words and actions.

Sedition – if that was what Lieutenant Sallis intended – was after all extremely hard a charge to prove, as Major Templar had informed him, when they had indulged in a hypothetical chat on the subject.

★ ★ ★

Alex was exhausted. The action he had seen in the Somme offensive had been a gruelling experience since July and the Devonshire Regiment had suffered significant losses. He had tried putting events behind him, with limited success, and he still felt a pang of guilt, whenever he thought about Eloise, however fleetingly. Many of his comrades urged him to relax, about their encounter, but he couldn't, Alex just knew he wasn't made that way.

He couldn't brush off the reality that he may have betrayed Laura, by being with Eloise, even if he had been too inebriated to remember much detail. Part of him wanted to see her again, to confront her about what they had done, but he also feared another encounter, in case the truth of what she had to tell him was too awful to bear, and that once he knew he would be unable to face Laura. He had *desired* Eloise, he couldn't deny it, and that feeling was for him the most damning evidence of his betrayal with which he couldn't reconcile. One volunteer private in whom he had confided, had been very dismissive, when Alex described Eloise, who he too had been treated by.

'If you went with her and couldn't remember, it probably didn't happen,'

'I'm telling you I woke up naked in her bed.'

'So, she undressed you and lent you her bed for the night. I guess that anything more is just your fantasy. A nice one to have, but a fantasy all the same.'

Alex had said no more as the volunteer was projecting envy, which Alex understood, but he was convinced, because everything Eloise had said to him the morning after, implied they had been intimate and the evidence supported her claim. What's more she had derived *pleasure* from their encounter and felt no obligation to conceal it. She had no regrets, leaving the self-torment to him.

The Devonshire Regiment continued to hold their position against heavy constant enemy bombardment, while the CO felt that Alex had turned a corner and was demonstrating once again, his early promise, as a soldier who could be relied upon. The promotion to Lance Corporal had been made he was told on merit, as much as on expediency as they needed competent and confident soldiers, who went above and beyond the call of duty. Alex needed convincing that he fell into this category, and initially the claim had caused him to laugh mirthlessly. If they only knew how tormented I feel inside, he thought dismally. Nonetheless he was satisfied with how he had adjusted to life in the trenches. He often thought about Laura at fleeting moments, at home in Covington, and when the time allowed he wrote her long detailed letters, trying not to alarm her by making life in the trenches sound as dismal as the reality often was.

One morning in late October, he woke, his sleep interrupted at regular intervals, by enemy shelling. Turning to his right, he nudged a comrade gently in the ribs, not realising at first that his comrade was a corpse, and then he saw a large rat scurrying upwards towards the corpse's chest. Positioning his rifle, making as little sound as he could, he speared the rodent with his bayonet, tossing it away. Vermin were another unpleasant reality of life in the trenches that he had felt it wise to spare Laura from. Reaching over, he checked there was no sign of breathing and closed his eyes. Taking a deep breath, he composed himself. Seeing death at such close quarters on a daily basis hadn't come any easier and he never wanted it to.

'Don't feel it too much,' he admonished himself as he wiped a stray tear away. He could barely feel anything in his hands from the cold and his khaki overcoat offered little protection, while the rain which had been incessant for weeks, had finally given them some reprieve. Holding their position with ever diminishing resources was hard, but they had no choice but to *endure,* but for how much longer he wondered desperately.

★ ★ ★

The relationship between Daniel and Lieutenant Sallis was deteriorating rapidly. Sallis didn't like him, and he now showed no inclination to hide the fact. Daniel could live with the man's obvious antipathy, but the lack of respect for his rank, he wouldn't tolerate. The Lieutenant had no more respect for those in ranks below him, despite what he described as his *"man of the people"* credentials. He questioned routine orders at will and Daniel was convinced, that it must be part of some plan or plot, but to achieve what he didn't know, unless of course, sedition was exactly what Sallis had in mind. It made no difference. He wasn't going to be cowed by this man, and having Major Templar as his CO helped, although that fact was likely to induce a sneer of derision from Sallis as Major Templar had been a friend of Daniel's father for many years, and thus he represented everything that Sallis held in contempt.

Major Templar had been a guest at his wedding to Lavinia, and he knew Lieutenant Fearns, and was aware of the contribution he had made to the war until he had been invalided out. Sitting in his dug-out Daniel was worrying about how to begin another difficult letter to the family of a volunteer, who had died in action within a fortnight of being sent to the Front. He felt a shadow over him and looking up he saw Corporal Broom standing there, with a sombre look on his face.

'We've had reports of desertion, Sir.'

'From our battalion?' Daniel asked, throwing down his pen. Desertion was as big a problem as losses suffered in action, but desertion amounted to a sense of shame. Convicted it meant death by firing squad. How did you *write* that letter to a grieving family? Much easier to say their loved one had died in action. A hero.

Corporal Broom inclined his head with a half nod. The solemnity of the situation was etched into his expression.

'Have they been apprehended?'

'Yes Sir, and are under arrest. But Sir, the most alarming aspect is that, it has been reported to me, is the line of defence for their actions.'

Daniel jumped up. His brows pleated in a deep frown. 'Which is?'

'One of our two is saying he was actively encouraged to run for it. Assured by this person that he could see to it, that they would look the other way and that if he knew of any other potential deserters that he should encourage them also to do as their *"conscience"* bid them.'

'Is the deserter giving us a name? Is his claim credible?'

'Yes Sir, In both instances. The 'deserter' is stating that he was actively encouraged to *desert* and that it came from Lieutenant Sallis.' Corporal Broom bowed his head. His tone was grave, almost as if he was reporting more heavy losses, and Daniel understood his embarrassment and his lack of credulity.

It was impossible to believe at face value and in most cases he would dismiss it immediately as a pathetic plea for mitigation, but with Lieutenant Sallis he had come to believe just about anything, and that is why in his gut, he believed the deserter could be telling the *truth*.

As a motivation for desertion and for the shame in being caught it was too incredible, but he was still inclined towards caution, despite the pernicious influence of Sallis; it had to be managed with deftness and diplomacy. Daniel lit a cigarette and drew heavily on it. He paced the floor and after minutes of silence, which must have seemed longer to Broom, he said, 'Does the deserter think that sharing this will mean he's spared the firing squad?'

'I can't say, Sir.'

Daniel grimaced. His personal view of Sallis, aside, if the deserter was deemed a credible witness his claim amounted to an incitement to treason on Sallis's part. He didn't condone desertion by any means, but he had seen for himself that some of the recruits since conscription were woefully ill-equipped emotionally, to cope with life in the trenches. Desertion was invariably the last act of desperate naïve young men, sometimes no more than boys, but what if these two had been encouraged, and that the man responsible for that *incitement* was his second-in-command?

Daniel nodded at Broom. 'Leave it with me, Corporal, and thanks for letting me know.'

Saluting, Corporal Broom left Daniel alone in the dug-out. Daniel looked at the blank sheet that was to be the letter he was about to write to the family of a brave volunteer killed in action and he couldn't help smiling at the irony. The deserter, informed of what he faced, if found guilty of desertion, would have no motive for inventing such a story. Accusing an officer would hardly see him being spared the firing squad. So why do it? It was just too incredible. He would have to tread very carefully, dealing with this, and reporting the facts to Major Templar would require all the diplomatic skills he possessed. Objectivity was key. He couldn't allow it to appear personal against Sallis, but Daniel knew that if fortune was ever going to present him with the opportunity to be rid of Sallis and *his* pernicious influence then this was surely it.

He had hoped for such a moment where Sallis would over-reach himself, but he was no fool, and Daniel would have to treat him with the same respect, so as not to alert him, but he could hope that arrogance would be the Lieutenant's ultimate failing.

Daniel sent a message to Major Templar, handing it to a volunteer with the strict orders that it should be handed personally to the Major at HQ. He exhaled on a deep breath, confident that he was taking the only action he could as an officer, with the information he had. He hoped he wasn't being played for a fool and this whole story wasn't some kind of trap; to spare another disillusioned boy from the firing squad and his family from the shame of desertion was his duty, and one that he wouldn't shirk.

★ ★ ★

The message summoning Daniel to HQ came two days later. Although he had no idea what was developing, Lieutenant Sallis was sceptical of the need for Daniel to go to HQ and he bluntly told him so. 'You're needed here with respect Sir.' Daniel never ceased to be surprised that Sallis could use the word respect without ever meaning it. 'With respect Lieutenant, I am required to attend HQ on the orders of Major Templar. It would do you no harm to follow my example, rather than second guess every instruction given to you.'

Sallis sneered, 'I doubt I will ever follow your example in anything Sir.'

'As you wish, but remember this, while you're here, you are under my command so as a courtesy, I am telling you that I am being driven to HQ and how long I shall be detained for, I couldn't say. You are in charge.'

'But still you don't know why?'

Daniel suppressed a smile. 'When you have a need to know Lieutenant I will see to it that you're kept informed.'

'So there *is* going to be a push? At last, an all-out assault on the enemy's position.' Sallis grinned, and Daniel thought the man's appetite for spilling other's blood was nauseous.

'I repeat Lieutenant. A need to know basis and when you need to know what Major Templar has planned you will be informed.'

Daniel didn't wait for a salute, with his cap and swagger stick in hand, he shouldered his way past Sallis to the staff car, turning to say, 'Return to your post Lieutenant Sallis. The men are relying on you. *Don't* let them down!'

Major Templar's Office – Command HQ

'It's preposterous! I can barely believe it!' Major Templar was a man of his father's generation and the Major's reaction was much like how Daniel would expect the Earl would react if he were presented with the same facts. Albeit with considerably more bluster. Daniel knew how difficult it was to comprehend as he was also mindful that any soldier caught trying to desert would seek mitigation for their actions.

'So you're inclined to believe this volunteer? He's not trying to divert attention in the hope of saving his neck?'

'He was caught in the act of deserting his post, Major. He must know he has no defence against that charge, and he has no reason to believe that making such a claim would save him from the firing squad. So why make it?'

Major Templar nodded, opening the file of reports he read them through minutely.

'According to this Sallis has an impeccable record. I'm dashed if I can *understand* what his motives might be. I can't Daniel. I just can't.'

'He might not have been caught before. Not implicated. Corporal Broom reported to me what he had heard and the deserter claims he was actively encouraged to desert and to take as many volunteers as he could with him. An orchestrated manoeuvre designed to debilitate troop numbers, and weaken morale.'

'But as the deserter was caught?'

'The risk was all his. Sallis would have a win either way. If one deserter got away, his plan worked, but if they were caught he would be confident their claim would be trashed, their credibility undermined. Which means that many a potential deserter might be reluctant to speak, out, and they always have their own reasons for deserting which for MPs is usually enough.'

Templar shook his head; standing up he paced the floor, in an agitated state, slapping the folder against his thigh.

'I can't believe it and I won't! We would be setting a precedent here, that a deserter might start believing they will be let off if they could prove there was incitement. You have to admit Captain Swiffen that you are slightly prejudiced against Lieutenant Sallis, probably with good reason, and that might be his line of defence.'

Daniel nodded slowly, the sinking feeling that the chance of ridding himself of Sallis might still be denied. 'I think it is fair to point out Major that Lieutenant Sallis has a much deeper issue with me, than I have with him, his appetite for blatant insubordination aside.'

'You would trust Corporal Broom?'

'Completely Sir.'

Templar nodded. 'Broom is a good man. Solid. I've seen as much for myself. Well thank you for bringing this matter to my attention. We need proof to proceed with this though, which is why I am inclined to instruct a delay in proceeding to firing squad. I want to be present when the deserter is interrogated. If I am convinced then that there is sufficient evidence that Lieutenant Sallis is inciting men to desert, I shall act.'

Daniel took the last mouthful of the small brandy that Major Templar had insisted he have, in a gulp and with a nonchalant shrug. He knew Major Templar well enough to realise that the decision he had made was the best that *he* could have hoped for, but he couldn't help thinking as he left HQ and climbed back into the car, that a metaphorical rug had been pulled from under him, and despite being guilty of a treasonable act, Lieutenant Sallis might yet had secured himself a moral victory.

★ ★ ★

As the days rolled by, October gave way to November and the rain continued and intensified. The resulting mud becoming as much an enemy as the troops on the other side of No Man's Land. The fighting was as intense as ever and morale among the Devonshire volunteers, dipped alarmingly. Despite this they continued to hold firm in their position, but Alex was one of many claiming exhaustion. One of his comrades suggested in jest that he was pining for Nurse Chagal. Alex took the teasing in good faith, but his spirits remained low. For days the action at Ancre raged, as the enemy lines remained resolutely robust and the British tried for a 'big push'. Ancre would be one of the last big battles of the Somme offensive which had begun in the golden hue of summer, in July, and even allowing for the heavy losses suffered on the first day, nothing could compare with the poor level of morale, being felt now. Even the intervening months, which had continued to see confidence sapping losses and the added burden of beastly weather conspired to haemorrhage troops of their hope that a reprieve was in sight.

Into this bleakness Alex was becoming a man that younger recruits looked upto for confidence and reassurance. He was disillusioned by the fact that mostly he had nothing to offer them. He had been in action now for eighteen months as the war passed its second anniversary and would likely see its third Christmas. There were occasions when even a minor injury, that took you out of the trenches and into the relative safety of the CCS was to be welcomed, and Alex had seen his share of those makeshift marquees with row upon row of identical beds occupied by broken young men who'd had their fill of irregular rations and a merciless lack of sleep. He had no wish to return to one of them but he still had an urge to see Nurse Chagal again. Perhaps to assuage himself of guilt. He wanted to *demand* the truth from her, and put to rest the gnawing doubt that he could even unwittingly have betrayed Laura.

Nurse Chagal had the power to arouse lust in the men who came into her care, because they were far from home and missing their sweethearts. It enraged Alex that he couldn't be different from the others. That he was no stronger than those comrades on weekend leave who had abandoned him to Nurse Chagal's care so they could avail themselves of the local whores on the night he was tricked into her bed. Although he had to admit he hadn't been able to rationalise his reaction to Lieutenant Swiffen either, and their encounter had been all too fleeting.

'You're missing Laura.' He told himself and pulling out the worn sepia photograph he ran his thumb over it. Seeing her face always made him smile, because he could imagine what it would be like to encircle her waist with his hands, to gently cup her cheek and look for the dancing merriment in her eyes as he bestowed a kiss on her cheek or forehead, before kissing her more deeply, hungrily on the mouth.

It was Laura. Always her that should be dominating his thoughts. The focus of his attention. Laura. The only girl he had ever wanted. The girl he had vowed he would go home to and claim as his bride. Laura, who he was absolutely determined to stay alive for, so that he would see her again.

★ ★ ★

When reports that another conscript to the Hertfordshire Regiment had been caught attempting to desert reached Daniel, he immediately leapt to the conclusion that Sallis was behind it, without any accusation being made, and although Corporal Broom urged him to be cautious, Daniel struggled to contain his anger. Banging his fist against the table in his dug-out, he lit a cigarette, drawing heavily on it, as he tried to dissipate his anger. Major Templar had been implicit in his warnings not to alert Sallis to the fact they were investigating him, so after a few calming drags on his cigarette, Daniel decided to heed Broom's advice and in thanking the Corporal he tried concealing his disappointment.

'You know it's possible the other deserter who suggested Sallis had coerced him, may have misinterpreted the Lieutenant's words.'

Daniel shot him a quick glance and Broom held up his hands in mock surrender. 'I'm just saying it is going to be hard to prove it. I want rid of Sallis as much as anyone Sir.'

Daniel nodded, acknowledging his Corporal had a point. Broom had demonstrated his worth in the trenches more than once and as much as Daniel would like to nail Sallis, bringing him down on the word of men caught in the act of deserting their post would be controversial unless Sallis grew complacent, and began making errors, or he became too brazen in his efforts. He still couldn't work out the Lieutenant's motive, unless he truly was a seditionist, hell bent on inciting mutiny in the ranks.

Sallis made no secret of his trenchant political views, and Daniel knew how much the Lieutenant disapproved of the "privileged class" into which he had been born, about which Sallis had been scathing. Daniel stubbed out his cigarette, mumbling, 'So I must bide my time.'

'Wait to see what the Major comes up with. Morale is bound to be low Sir. Losses have been considerable and most of newest recruits face the prospect of their first Christmas at the Front and, unlike last year, when most of them were volunteers, we now have conscripts who had no choice but to enlist. If Lieutenant Sallis is involved as we've been led to believe, some of our recruits won't have needed much persuasion.'

Daniel smiled. 'Thank you Corporal.' At the moment the Corporal saluted and took his leave, Lieutenant Sallis appeared in the entrance to the dug-out. Sneering derisorily, his resentment of Daniel, evident, he asked, 'Something wrong Captain?'

'You could say that Lieutenant. The Corporal was informing me that another of our conscripts has been caught attempting to desert their post. It is becoming an epidemic.'

'Can you blame them Sir? Young rookies out of their depth. Some of them just boys who've barely started shaving, and yet they get minimum training, meagre rations, they have a rifle thrust into their hands and are instructed to fight. All at the behest of our spineless and "not so Liberal Government". Come and kill or be killed in the name of the Empire, in this hellhole or face imprisonment and accusations of cowardice. Who wouldn't be tempted?'

'I haven't been tempted Lieutenant, nor have you, or Corporal Broom, and we all share the same fate.'

Sallis thought for a moment, his expression blank, and then he said, 'Yes Sir, but as I said, we're men, most of the "so-called" deserters are mere boys.'

Daniel knew he was getting nowhere. A man of Sallis's

cunning, was too shrewd to let anything slip easily. They would have to get the evidence that he was inciting desertion; hard proof he wouldn't be able to deny. Daniel could only hope that Major Templar was making progress.

★ ★ ★

Three days later Alex was becoming impatient and slightly restless, eager to see more action. He volunteered for night patrol whenever the opportunity arose. Boredom had become his biggest concern, as lethal to his state of mind, as his fear of the enemy. His sergeant said he needed to be carefully watched, as did the CO.

A reckless soldier was as much a liability as one who had lost their nerve and they didn't need either. At times he could appear pensive but at others more than ready for the final push in the Battle of Ancre. That morning other soldiers had noticed the change in Alex's mood and one of the men saw an opportunity to bait him even more with a careless remark. 'Even if you're wounded Lance-Corporal, there's a chance you might be reunited with that gorgeous French nurse of yours.'

Alex was about to go at him, with fists flying, until a sergeant intervened. 'What is it with you Conyer? You're so fired up, you'll go into combat with anyone. Just calm yourself, conserve your energies for when the order comes to go over the top, and please consign yourselves to fighting the enemy, not among yourselves. Ok?'

The Sergeant gave Conyer a warning look and left. When the order finally came to go 'over the top', Alex felt as tightly wound as a coiled spring. He was up into No Man's Land and into a hail of enemy shelling and when a comrade next to him, took a hit, Alex took out the assailant and went further towards the enemy lines, despite the warning calls from behind him. He was firing rapidly but indiscriminately and then suddenly his vision was blurred. He felt his legs wouldn't move and the blue-grey smoke of gunfire was replaced by a wall of white, and that was the moment, that he stopped seeing and remembering. Anything.

★ ★ ★

Daniel used the time before receiving orders to go 'over the top' writing to Lavinia, but it was proving one of the hardest letters he had penned, because, for the first time in awhile, he feared it might be the last he would get to write. They had been told it was to be a final push to bring the months long Somme offensive to a conclusion, and he feared that if she wasn't already with child, the long unbroken line of succession enjoyed by the Earls of Royston would come swiftly to an end. He smiled wryly, taking a quick drag on his cigarette, it wasn't the first time he had predicted his demise, but he hadn't felt this level of apprehension and despondency in weeks. He had to survive. There was no alternative. Although he had lived all his life, reminded of the burden of duty as the eldest son, he had always accepted it as the constant in his life. The wretched war had compelled him to seek a wife more urgently than otherwise would have been necessary, but he felt there was a cloud of expectation hanging over him now, to ensure he came home from the war unscathed. There was he knew second cousins who could inherit his title and the estate, however, the reality struck him that as an outcome he would feel cheated. He realised in that dimly lit dug-out as sporadic shelling droned on above him, that perhaps for the first time since childhood, he wasn't burdened by the responsibility. He wanted to claim his birthright. He wanted to survive this push against the enemy and every other offensive until this bloody war ended.

He was sealing the envelope for his letter to Lavinia, when a private came into the dug-out, and, after saluting, handed him the message from High Command. Its contents were stark. There was as yet no irrefutable evidence to support the charge that Lieutenant Sallis was inciting new recruits to desert. Daniel was almost blinded by rage. He screwed the message into a ball, tossing it aside, to the dismay of the private who had brought it. Daniel turned to him. 'Anything else? No other messages?'

The private shook his head. 'Dismissed,' Daniel said curtly. He removed his revolver from its holster, checked it, and grabbing his swagger stick, and helmet tucked under his arm, he strode out to the trench. The mood of his men was hard to gauge, some were their usual boisterous selves,while others grew quiet, pensive when the time to go over the top drew nearer and the time for personal reflection grew stronger.

It was the final push which had been talked about for days and some were more eager than others to get started. He was in two minds, but as Daniel looked down the line and saw Sallis, he could see there was no doubt the Lieutenant was pumped up. Here was a man who had never backed away from a fight in his life; one might even say he relished it. The man was a bully with a huge chip on his shoulder, and proof or not, Daniel was convinced his Lieutenant was involved.

Sallis approached him as he made his way along the trench. 'Are we ready for the final word to go over Captain?'

'Not yet. I'm just checking the men are ready for it, when the word comes.'

'With respect Sir, I noticed a private bringing you a message. Was that not the instructions to go over the top?'

Daniel half-turned, looking Sallis squarely in the face. 'No, that was a personal message for me from the Major.'

'Personal, private what is all this? Surely the men who are going to risk their necks going over the top have the right to know what's bloody going on.'

'I don't care for your tone Lieutenant Sallis. Nor do I

appreciate whatever it is you are implying. I have told you, that I have not as yet received the command to attack. You will have to be patient.'

Daniel turned his back then and he heard Sallis sneer. 'You'll forgive me Sir, when I say I don't believe you. I shouldn't be surprised that you're holding out on us. It's typical of you and your rotten bloody class!' Daniel turned sharply, ignoring the shocked intake of breath, from the men around him, astounded by the Lieutenant's insolence. He felt his hand on the revolver, slightly moist from his sweat, and with gritted teeth he looked Sallis squarely in the eyes, holding his gaze. From the corner of his eyes he saw Corporal Broom shaking his head slowly, warning him not to act rashly, but he couldn't back down. He couldn't let Sallis win.

'What class would that be Lieutenant?'

'The "privileged class". To which you and the Major belong. Have these plans for the final push been cosily hatched between you two as they would have at Eton?'

Daniel laughed. Sallis sounded pathetic! A man convinced of a sense of injustice, and evidently of low self-esteem. 'So what class do you belong to Lieutenant?'

'I'm working class! Proud to be so. Like most of the men in the trenches, our lives dependent upon the word of our so-called masters. Men like you Captain.'

'Or is it the traitors' class you belong to? Is that why you have been inciting men to desert their post. Is that your motive Lieutenant, to invoke mutiny among the ranks?'

Sallis kept his expression blank, his face inches away from Daniel's. There was an audible expression of disbelief from the men around them. Incredulous at what they were witnessing.

'I have no idea what you're talking about Sir. Why would I be inciting a mutiny? I know the penalty for desertion. Why would I incite that?'

'To teach my class – the "privileged" class as you call it–

a lesson. To stir up trouble, encourage an atmosphere of resentment among the ranks. That's your particular skill isn't it Sallis? Undermining authority.'

'So where's all this coming from Sir? Where is your proof, or is it all a figment of your expensively cultivated imagination?'

Daniel smiled. Sallis was just jealous of what others had. A little man, more weighed down by his lack of self-worth, than by a lack of opportunity. He had come across many good men of varying backgrounds since arriving in France, but none were as soulless as Lieutenant Sallis.

'I have received sufficient intelligence that you've been exploiting the fears of the youngest recruits. Told them that if they were inclined to desert you would look the other way and should they get caught you would simply say they misunderstood. Desperate men will say almost anything to avoid the firing squad and should they escape, well that would be mission accomplished.'

Sallis smiled broadly. 'With respect Sir.' He almost spat the word respect contemptuously in Daniel's face, and coming closer, he said, 'I think you might be losing the plot Sir!'

Daniel saw the red mist of rage before his eyes, and pulling his revolver from its holster and cocking it, he pushed the barrel under Sallis's chin, to the gasped horror of the men in their immediate vicinity. Corporal Broom tried moving closer to intervene, but his path was blocked.

'Give me one good reason why I shouldn't pull this trigger and blow your miserable brains out, with respect Lieutenant?'

For the first time since Sallis had been sent as a replacement for Lieutenant Fearns, Daniel saw fear in his eyes. He exerted another inch of pressure on the barrel and Sallis's head fell back.

Daniel raised a quizzical eyebrow, encouraging Sallis to respond, which he did with a croak, 'Because it would amount to murder Sir.'

'He's right Captain. You're better than this.' Said Broom hesitantly.

'Thank you for saying so Corporal, but the Lieutenant doesn't agree. I belong to a rotten privileged class as far as he is concerned. My defence would be that I was provoked, claim temporary insanity, blame it on battle fatigue. Either way you would still be dead Sallis.'

'You would probably get away with it as well Sir. I daresay the Old Boys' Network would rally round to cover your back. Isn't Major Templar a friend of the family? An old Etonian as well I should imagine.'

'I wouldn't have to cover his back because Captain Swiffen isn't going to shoot you! Remove your revolver Captain. Now!'

Daniel turned to see Major Templar and he exhaled a deep breath of relief, as he feared that he might well have shot the miserable man. He eased the revolver away from Sallis's chin . Then bowed his head.

'Corporal Broom please arrest Lieutenant Sallis,' the Major instructed.

'Arrest me? This bloody madman held a revolver against me! This is a rotten stitch-up!'

Some of the men spoke in agreement. Major Templar silenced them. 'Be quiet! Lieutenant Sallis you are under arrest for incitement to treason. We have sufficient evidence to support the claim of one, perhaps two recruits, caught in the act of desertion that they acted on your specific encouragement.' Major Templar approached Sallis, looked at him with disgust, and in return Sallis indicated his contempt. 'Take him away,' he instructed the two military policemen he had brought with him.

Templar approached Daniel, he held out his hand palm upwards, nodding at the revolver. Daniel, his face suffused with embarrassment, handed it to the Major, who gave it to Corporal Broom. 'You're in charge for the time being.'

The Major patted Daniel on the shoulder as he led him into

the dug-out. There were a few random grunts of disapproval, but nothing serious. Daniel had earned the respect of the men in his battalion, but whether he still commanded it after this was in doubt.

Seated in the dug-out the Major shook his head. The silence was deafening until he spoke. 'I specifically said await my instructions regarding Sallis. I can't begin to tell you how disappointed I am Captain Swiffen. Show some discipline. I know you have it in you to be a fine officer, but there's precious little evidence of it tonight. It would have been murder, if you had pulled that trigger!'

Daniel laughed mirthlessly, but a stern look from Major Templar, discouraged him from going further. 'I fail to see what you find amusing about this fiasco.'

'If I had been given the order to send the men over the top and Sallis had been shot dead, it would be ok for me to be relieved at his loss, even glad, but having the desire to do it myself amounts to murder. That is somewhat ironic!'

'From what I witnessed had Sallis been shot by enemy fire, his death would be no great loss to the Allied cause, but you being court-martialled for murder most definitely would. Despite the drivel Sallis was talking about me having your back, and attempting to cover it up, I wouldn't even try with so many witnesses.'

Daniel bowed his head. He lit a cigarette with trembling fingers, as the enormity of what he had been so close to doing, really began to sink in. 'I'm sorry Major. There's no excuse I know, but I saw the red mist of anger and acted on what… impulse.'

Major Templar's expression was grim. He nodded. 'Yes and in the most undisciplined manner that an officer of your calibre could.'

'So, what changed suddenly? Your message said there wasn't enough evidence with which to challenge him.'

'Until another deserter said he had been actively encouraged. Apparently he was told it would teach the top brass a lesson. Especially if the number of desertions escalated dramatically, as that along with the losses would further demoralise morale, so the Army would have to disguise the burden of loss through desertion or risk compromising the integrity of how we're fighting the war.'

'So Sallis wanted to orchestrate a campaign of mass desertion?'

Major Templar remained tight-lipped. Steepling his fingers, against pursed lips he blew air into his cheeks. 'It's all still aimless conjecture until we've interviewed him formally, but in theory, yes that could have been his intention. War does strange things to some men and you were very sceptical of the value of your contribution when you arrived. I think Sallis is a weak man who has let his political views rule him and thus he has lost perspective. Let's forget Sallis. I am granting you at least two weeks' leave, maybe even three, if I can swing it. After which I want you to attend a Medical Board.'

He held up his hand to quell Daniel's protest, adding, 'No argument Captain Swiffen. After tonight I'm not having you back until you have been passed mentally fit for action. Go home to Lavinia and after that I strongly recommend Craiglockhart Hospital, in Edinburgh. There are some splendid chaps there doing some remarkable work on the effects on the mind of fighting men. I am convinced you're suffering from combat fatigue and, I'm taking no chances. I want you back to being the Captain Swiffen, that I can rely upon. I saw the look in your eyes when you had that revolver against his chin. You wanted to kill him and with one careless slip you might have succeeded. So get your stuff together, I'm taking you back to HQ and you'll be on a troop ship home within days.'

Daniel smiled to himself as he set about the task. He knew the Major had his back, whether he deserved it or not, but he was grateful, because he realised just how close to the edge he had been. Pulled back from the precipice of disdain and social shame, which would have remained with him for years. For the fact that he had been teetering on that edge, at all was something for which he only had himself to blame.

14

Alex had little memory of anything after he blundered into combat with the enemy and was fortunate to be rescued by a comrade. It had been the last great push of the Somme offensive and he had been at the heart of it, according to what he had been told. For hours he had veered between life and death, but they had saved him. The doctors had done their work, but it appeared – somewhat ironically – that the person to whom he owed most thanks was Nurse Chagal. She had been due to end her secondment at the CCS but the heavy losses suffered during the final push, meant her return had to be delayed, due to her stubborn refusal to leave until Alex was past the worst. The decision inevitably earned her another negative comment on her record, exacerbated by her threat to resign if she were coerced into moving on.

It was a serious dilemma for Sister Hopkins to deal with and not one she relished, however, for the time being, Eloise got her way. She had done double shifts, back-to-back, and once she was forced to go home in exhaustion after a senior nurse caught her at the start of a morning shift asleep on folded arms, half lying on Alex's bed: she had put a cold flannel against his forehead, to reduce his fever and redressed his wounds. Sister Hopkins had lost count of the times she had cautioned Nurse Chagal for becoming too attached to one patient, but her warnings were proving futile. It was obvious to most of her medical colleagues and the other patients that she didn't care for Lance-Corporal Conyer, as she would any other patient. She cared for him, as she would a lover. In a busy CCS which was understaffed and burdened by an endless flow of new casualties, the Sister hadn't the energy to discipline Nurse Chagal, as she would have done in a civilian hospital. She was too good at what she did to have the luxury of losing her, even if the MO who had noticed Nurse Chagal's emotional over-dependency on Lance-Corporal Conyer and had insisted action be taken.

'You're a very lucky young man Lance-Corporal. We came very close to losing you, more than once.'

Alex had smiled wanly, avoiding Eloise's gaze. He turned instead to look at the Doctor standing beside her. 'So you can pass me fit to return to action?'

The doctor shook his head. 'Not me, your CO maybe, but I have assured him that for the time being, you won't be going anywhere, other than the Field Hospital, to which you will be transferred for further treatment. This would have happened sooner, had you not relapsed. The paperwork for your transfer is, I believe, in hand.'

Alex nodded. 'The comrade I attempted to save, did he make it?'

The doctor looked at Nurse Chagal, who dipped her head. 'Sadly not.' His tone was flat, some might have said cold.

'So I suffered for nothing?'

The doctor stepped forward and said, 'You acted very courageously. Some might say too rashly in defence of your comrades and that's nothing to regret. Indeed your bravery in attempting to save him, might have been in vain, but please remember Lance-Corporal, that another man's bravery is the reason you're lying here now.'

The doctor wrote something on Alex's notes and replaced the file at the foot of the bed, he then looked quizzically at another file under his arm. 'Why do I have this?' he asked irritably, his brows pleated in a deep frown. Sister Hopkins appeared at his side and took the file. 'I don't understand how this could have happened again. I apologise doctor, this file is for Private Connor. I do wish the orderlies would pay more attention to what they are reading.'

'You will have to remind them Sister. We cannot afford to let the patients' files be mixed up.' He completed his rounds and Sister Hopkins summoned Nurse Chagal to her office.

'Your secondment here is now coming to an end, Nurse, and in light of recent events, I can't be sorry. Your conduct in respect of Lance-Corporal Conyer has been totally unprofessional and it was completely unacceptable for you to threaten resignation to delay your transfer. I have given you more leeway than I ever would to any junior in civilian circumstances, but your attention to him has come at the detriment of other patients. Thankfully, as Dr Crossley has explained, Lance-Corporal Conyer is to be transferred to the Field Hospital. Which one is not yet decided but should it be Etaples, I am thankful that your presence there as well will soon become someone else's problem. Please return to your duties and endeavour not to compel me to summon you back in here on your last shift. Please send the orderly responsible for the patient file mix-up to see me.'

Nurse Chagal stifled a smile and half bowing she left.

CCS – France, two days later.

When the instruction came for Alex to be transferred to the Field Hospital at Etaples for further treatment, he was relieved to leaving at last, but disappointed the doctor had acquiesced to the plan that Eloise be assigned to accompany him, as his personal nurse. She vehemently denied that assertion of course, saying it made sense as her secondment at the CCS was over, and she had been transferred back to Etaples.

He had heard the rumours that Nurse Chagal was being sent back in disgrace. That the Sister could have kept her had she wished, but he knew how malicious gossip could spread and the orderlies had a particular talent for stirring trouble, especially when it deflected blame for their own errors.

One orderly had boldly confided to him that he had tried his luck with Nurse Chagal and had been brutally rebuffed. She was accused by orderlies and fellow nurses of being cold and aloof. Alex knew better, but he kept his counsel. Eloise had deceived him about the events of the night she had lent him her bed, he was convinced of that, and he owed her no favours. He had heard about how much effort she had put into looking after him, but she was a trained nurse, that was her job. He wasn't going to deny that he had desired her sexually, but he had done nothing to encourage her obsession with him. That was a creation of her imagination and she could claim ownership of it.

He had tried finding out where he would go after his time at the Field Hospital, but the MO was being deliberately evasive. He had come to realise that Dr Crossley had a particular talent for that. He longed to be sent home to his beloved Laura. It seemed like an eternity had passed since her last letter, and he hoped she was ok and managing to keep away from that brute Stoughton.

Doctor Crossley came to do the final rounds before formally releasing Alex from his care. The ambulances were on standby and five patients were being transferred to Etaples. Alex was surprised to learn that among them was Private Earol Connor of the Hertfordshire Regiment, who had he believed been deemed unfit to return to action, until the medical advice had been countermanded, and Connor had returned to the

Front, an emotional wreck who was more of a liability to his comrades, until a further injury had resulted in common sense being applied and he had been declared unfit to return to action. His war was finally over.

As they were being prepared for transfer to the ambulances, Dr Crossley shook Alex's hand, wishing him good luck, handing the relevant files to an orderly, instructing him to follow. One orderly looked confused until a colleague instructed him to leave the files with the patients and to send them out to the waiting ambulances. The rookie orderly did as he was bidden, watching the stretcher bearers carry patients out.

Alex felt relieved that he wouldn't see the inside of this marquee and the CCS again, but was far from certain he had seen the last of his action in France. For the time being though, he was grateful for this brief hint of reprieve.

Covington, Devonshire – November, 1916

In the long hours of waiting afterwards, Laura wished her father hadn't witnessed the argument between her and Stoughton. She had always been able to handle the brutish head porter's unwelcome advances, and she would have done so again, without his intervention. Although the doctor went on to assure her that the altercation had little impact upon her father's fate and may only have delayed it, until another day.

She had been working at the range, preparing the evening meal, when she was approached from behind, feeling two big sweaty hands clasped around her waist. The breath on the back of her neck, with its stench of stale beer; she knew who it was and turning sharply, she swung the saucepan she held in her left hand, it only just missed him, landing a glancing blow, but it only served to embolden him, and he laughed.

'Playing hard to get are we? Should it make it interesting

and all the more fun when you finally succumb. Which you will. We may even laugh about it afterwards, when you're in my arms and my bed.'

'Never! You're mad!' shrieked Laura as she swung at him again. This time Stoughton managed to duck, before lunging to grab her once more, forcing Laura to push him away. In that moment, they both heard the lash of a whip, catching Stoughton's cheek and drawing blood; he thought Laura had struck him, but turning around he saw George Weston standing behind him, the whip in his hand and a face like thunder.

'I've told you before to keep your filthy hands off Laura but you don't listen. You never do, so you've had your last chance. No more warnings you don't heed.' George swung the whip again and Laura gasped in horror, as he struck Stoughton again, drawing blood on his other cheek.

'No Dad!' she shrieked but George wasn't listening, as the red mist of anger and resentment of Charlie Stoughton, built up over months, simmered over. Stoughton reached out to grab the whip before it lashed at him again, but he was too slow and it caught him on the thigh. He was much stronger and more agile than George, so when he grabbed for it again, the force threw George off his balance and he fell to the scullery floor, invoking a grin of triumph on Stoughton's face, as Laura went to her father's aide. The look of triumph faded swiftly as Stoughton saw George writhing on the floor, gripping his left arm, his face contorted in agony.

'What is it? I barely touched him!'

'Get help damn you! Quick!'

'That isn't my doing. He lost his balance.'

'Get help you oaf! It's serious.' Fighting back tears, Laura tried to soothe and reassure her father, keeping her worries at bay. A heart attack or maybe a stroke was all she could think, but for the moment all she had was hope.

To his credit Stoughton did act swiftly bringing someone

with medical training from the platform, who kept her father comfortable until an ambulance arrived, but it was taking an age and Laura was frantic that the delay might be crucial to her father's chances of recovery. She looked at the man whose expression was ashen, although he tried to appear positive. Her greatest fear, which had come unbidden the moment he had fallen, that her beloved father's life was going to ebb away on the scullery floor, was in danger of becoming a reality.

When George Weston was finally admitted into the small cottage hospital on the outskirts of Covington, their first expressions didn't give her much reason for hope. He had suffered a heart attack, it had been severe and it had left him terribly weak. Laura kept vigil at his bedside for seventy-two hours as he drifted in and out of consciousness. She couldn't recall having shed as many tears in her adult life as she did in that cold and sparse hospital ward. She wanted Alex and the fact she knew she couldn't have him with her now, saddened her all the more. When word got round that George Weston had been hospitalised the people of Covington rallied round. George Weston had been there for them at various points in their lives, so now when he and his lass needed help they would be there for them. In the weeks that followed, she would come to welcome their support, but for now all she wanted was for her beloved Dad to get well. Charlie Stoughton stayed away from the hospital, much to her relief and she feared now that he would be put in charge of running Covington Station, vowing that if did occur, she would have no choice, but to move out.

When the doctor came round to update her, saying George's heart was very weak, and that he was unlikely to survive beyond the week, she gave way under an onslaught of tears. Deep racking sobs, she feared might never cease, but they did and she held tightly onto his limp hand until the moment came when the doctor told her that he had gone and gently closed his eyes.

Laura walked home from the tiny cottage hospital with

the realisation that she was now an orphan slowly dawning on her, and that the only other person she really cared for was fighting in France and that his ultimate fate was as yet unclear. As the tears rolled unchecked down her cheeks that November evening, she knew with absolute certainty, that she had never felt quite so alone.

Field Hospital – Etaples, France

By the time the elementary error with patient files made by the orderly at the CCS became apparent, it was sadly too late for Private Connor. He was discovered on the second night, after instructions on file that he should be kept at Etaples, until medically cleared to return to action. So when this was relayed to him, he felt he had been deliberately tricked, as Dr Crossley had previously informed him that he was going home.

So desperate was he at the prospect of being sent back to the Front, he decided to take matters into his own hands. Stealing an orderly's razor which he concealed under his bed, he waited until darkness fell to slit both his wrists and bled to death.

For him a return to the Front was a far worse fate and one that he wasn't prepared to endure. His action was discovered when a red river of blood was seen seeping from his bedcovers. One orderly starting his shift shouted for help, and having glanced down at the file he shouted, 'It's Conyer! He's topped himself!'

Nurses ran to the bed pulling the screens around, as one nurse froze in response to what she had heard. Then she screamed uncontrollably, with grief. She could barely move until another nurse summoned her. 'Nurse Chagal? Are you ok? Come on, we need assistance.'

The Sister removed the blanket covering the soldier's face, and Nurse Chagal looked as if the colour had been bleached from hers. She felt nauseous, but she was overwhelmed because she knew from the first look that the pale face of the corpse was not Alex.

'This isn't Lance-Corporal Conyer!'

'What are you saying? This is his file!' The Sister stared at Nurse Chagal, waving the file in the air, adding, 'If you're in some sort of denial, I suggest you snap out of it. A patient has died at their own hand in our care. This is a serious matter.'

'Yes Sister, and I believe I know what has occurred.' She turned to the orderly, adding, 'Go to the next ward and find a patient with a file named Connor and bring that here. It will explain everything.'

The Sister was sceptical and for a moment Eloise doubted they would do as she bid them until the Sister, looking severe, nodded at the orderly and said flatly, 'Do it!'

When the orderly returned, he handed the file to the doctor who had just been summoned to attend the corpse of Private Connor. He looked at it and frowned. 'It will have to be verified, but I fear Nurse Chagal maybe correct. This file says the patient was to be kept here until he was shipped home. The file you found with this patient says he was to be treated here until fit for action. I spoke to this patient...' he turned towards the lifeless figure lying in the congealing pool of his blood, '... the one I now believe to be Private Connor, this morning and based the notes on that file. I can only imagine he feared he had been tricked. That there had been some change of plan, which motivated him to commit such a desperate act.'

'Exactly! Why would any soldier who knew he was being sent home resort to this after waiting so long?'

The sister still wasn't convinced, and Eloise was incandescent. 'If you're still not convinced call Dr Crossley at the CCS he will confirm that Private Connor was meant to be sent home. It's not the first time these patients files have been mixed up and he was furious the last time it happened.'

'I hope you're not suggesting the error was on the part of my staff, Nurse Chagal'

Eloise ignored her, although conscious that the reputation she had earned at the CCS, would have followed her back to Etaples. She didn't care though, she was just glad that Alex was alive.

'You had better be right Nurse Chagal,' said the Doctor grimly as he took the file marked Connor with him, indicating to the orderly that the river of blood should be dealt with.

The following day the mix-up was confirmed and flagged as an administrative error, although Dr Crossley was incandescent when informed that another mix-up over the same two patients' files had been allowed to occur again, adding that in his view the complacency of failure regarding the duty of care offered to Private Connor, was intolerable, resulting as it had in such fatal consequences. Although according to the MO at Etaples, Dr Crossley refused to accept blame, stating that he, like Eloise, suspected the latest error had taken place during transfer from the CCS. Eloise shared Dr Crossley's lack of confidence in the competence of some of their orderlies seconded to the CCS. A man had been allowed to die unnecessarily and the Field Hospital staff were simply attempting to cover their backs.

The mood on the ward where Connor had been was low after his death. That he was able to "borrow" a razor without it being noticed, was a serious breach of protocol. Alex, meanwhile, was informed that he was being sent home on a troop ship to Folkestone. He was confused by this development, but not complaining. A glance in the direction of Nurse Chagal warned her to say nothing; she didn't like deceiving him, but decided that it was easier to take the path of least resistance and she could do without yet another negative comment on her record. Parting from Alex was likely to wrench at her heart. She had struggled to reconcile herself to the reality that she was always likely to lose him to his beloved Laura eventually. She tucked the sheets in tighter and took his temperature, aware that her actions were being watched by the Sister.

'Is it true that Private Connor used a razor to slit his wrists?' Alex asked her, as she was about to leave. So the orderlies couldn't be discreet in that either? Why wasn't she surprised? So she inclined her head. 'Why now, when he had come so close to seeing the end of his war?'

'I guess it's difficult to understand the balance of a young man's mind. Especially one who had endured as much as Private Connor. He was always very troubled. I am only guessing, but perhaps he had just had enough, that this was his chance to escape and to seek the absolution, he had always wanted and yet somehow also feared. Please rest now. You have a long journey tomorrow.' Eloise gently patted the bed covers and blowing him a kiss, she walked away, ignoring the Sister's stern look, who pretended she hadn't noticed this latest gesture of over familiarity with a patient, but she said, 'Well done Nurse Chagal.'

'I didn't lie to him for you!' she said bluntly and despite the Sister's grim look she walked on through the corridor to a secluded corner, where hand against the wall, she wept silently; as the realisation hit her, that for the second time in her life, she had lost the man she dared to love.

Troop Ship to Folkestone – November, 1916

Alex approached the man tentatively, in case he wasn't recognised. 'Captain Swiffen?'

Daniel looked up and immediately he felt a reaction. For a moment he had thought about not acknowledging Alex, but it soon passed. Instead he raised a quizzical eyebrow prompting Alex to confirm.

'It is Lance-Corporal Conyer. Devonshire Regiment, although I was only a private the last time we met. You were directed to my bed at the CCS about a year ago.'

Daniel looked intensely at Alex and feeling his hand tremble slightly, he concealed it in his jacket pocket, tapping Alex on the shoulder instead. He had lost the boyish look he'd had Daniel thought, but he still didn't understand why this young man invoked the same reaction in him, each time they met.

'Of course Lance-Corporal. Please accept my apologies, but it has been awhile. So you have earned some home leave or is this the end for you?'

Alex shook his head. 'I don't know how I came to suddenly be granted leave. I was expecting to be laid up and bored at the Field Hospital at Etaples while they patched me up and then be sent back to the Front. Sadly it didn't end so well for Private Connor. I take it you're aware of what happened? The clerical errors over our files. The damned orderlies. Then they didn't even know he had grabbed one of their razors to top himself with.'

Alex watched as Daniel drew heavily on the stub of his cigarette, and then flicked it over the rail into the choppy waters of the Channel. Alex knew he was disregarding the request of staff at the Field Hospital not to divulge any details about Connor until the facts had been established, but he didn't care. If Connor's CO couldn't confirm that he had been passed unfit for action, then who could?

'I'm afraid I had more pressing matters to deal with at the time, but yes I was informed. It's a tragic case. I had previously argued that Private Connor should be declared unfit for action, and invalided out, but the command wouldn't hear of it. I can understand their rationale in a way. Our regiment suffered some heavy losses and there were several cases of desertion. Even so Connor was an emotional wreck. A liability to his comrades as much as anything, as his final act proves. You mustn't reproach yourself!'

Alex shook his head. 'I don't. The blame is on the orderlies who sent us to the Field Hospital at Etaples with the wrong files. Connor was signed off to go home. I was meant to return to action. I am convinced that when a doctor with no history of Connor's case related to him what had been written on my file, it tipped him over the edge.'

Daniel was astounded. 'You have proof of that?'

Alex shook his head. 'No but I'm convinced of it anyway. Let's face it, there's never an urge to admit human error. Connor stole a razor and used it on himself. No orderly bothered to report it missing. It's so much easier for medics to say he was unhinged. I believe he was betrayed.'

Alex took a deep breath, shaking his head. The wind hitting him in the face, causing his eyes to sting, he turned back and said. 'You could confirm that he was referred here!'

Daniel shook his head. 'I can't I'm afraid. It wasn't my decision. Private Connor was certainly let down. More than once. A casualty of war, I'm afraid and he is one of very many, but you cannot afford to make this your mission, without the risk of compromising yourself.'

Alex backed away, momentarily, shaking his head, but Daniel reached out for his hand. Suddenly they both felt the seismic connection and Daniel smiled. He couldn't have saved Private Connor, and he regretted that so much, but he wasn't going to stand by and let Lance-Corporal Conyer, be compromised, through his naivety, or by being too eager to prove a point, that would do him no favours in the long term. Especially when it was already too late for the man whose integrity he was seeking to preserve.

Daniel smiled slightly, feeling uneasy, he wanted to speak to Alex privately away from prying eyes and ears on this overcrowded troop ship and he was suddenly very grateful that

Major Templar had arranged for him to share a cabin, which was quite a coup on his part, although doubtless the mention of his title held some sway.

'Somehow I've managed to bag myself share of a cabin, where I have managed to secretly stash a rather good Cognac, if you are interested?' Daniel hoped there wasn't too much pleading in his tone, as he didn't want to appear desperate for the company of a Lance-Corporal, however, he had made no effort to make contact with anyone else on this overcrowded ship, and the man he was sharing the cabin with, another captain, was a 'crashing' bore, whom he felt no inclination to share anything with. He raised an eyebrow in encouragement and Alex nodded.

Taking a sheet from the notebook, he'd been writing in, Daniel wrote the cabin number down and folding the sheet, he slipped it into Alex's hand. 'Wait a couple of minutes, after I have gone and then follow me.'

He leaned closer, and whispered, 'Be as discreet as you can'

Alex was slightly bemused by Daniel's strenuous demand for discretion, after all what could be more normal than two comrades sharing a glass of Cognac or two, the disparity in their ranks notwithstanding. He guessed though that for a man like Daniel Swiffen, class would always be a consideration no matter the circumstances. He pocketed the sheet of paper and nodded, turning sharply to look at the starlit night and the choppy Channel waters. When he turned again, Daniel had made his departure.

Alex found Daniel's cabin quite easily, although the walk to it, earned him a few curious glances from the ship stewards. He knocked gently and when prompted to enter and close the door, Alex did as he was bidden, and Daniel thrust a glass of Cognac at him. He saw that he had also retrieved a slim hardback volume from his luggage, A Riot of Spring: A collection of Poems. His debut book, which he had speculated might have been a major literary triumph were it not for the outbreak of war. He handed a copy to Alex who looked at it quizzically.

'I'm not a great fan of poetry,' he said, sounding slightly guilty at the admission.

'It is a common enough response, especially from men.' In other circumstances, Daniel realised he might have added somewhat disparagingly, '... of a certain class,' but he held his tongue, smiling as he asked , 'Although you have a girlfriend, I recall at home?'

Alex nodded. 'Laura.'

'Then take it to read to her, for moments when you need to be romantic.'

Alex smiled uneasily, nodding at the empty chess board. 'No game tonight?'

'No. It belongs to the man I'm sharing this cabin with. He's eternally optimistic, that I will agree to a game but I'm not in the mood for chess. Do you play?'

For some reason he wanted Alex to surprise him. 'My grandfather did a little and he tried to get me to like it, but he never quite succeeded before he passed.'

'I'm sorry.' of Alex's confused look he added, 'You were very fond of him, I can tell. What did he do?'

'He was a stoker on Great Western Railways.'

Daniel smiled, pushing the book towards him. I've written a dedication to you, although I guess I should add your girl's name, as I daresay she will get most use of it. Then there's this letter. It's very brief, but if I may ask you one last favour, not to open it until after you have left the ship.'

Alex looked at him quizzically, 'How have you had time to write this?'

'I saw you were boarding, and I hoped we might get to meet, but a lot has happened since we met by chance at the CCS , and I wasn't absolutely certain you would remember me, so I wrote this on a whim, hoping I would get the chance to give it to you.'

Alex tentatively took the letter, shoving it into the pocket of his threadbare coat. He took a long gulp of Cognac, burning his throat. Then hesitantly he offered Daniel his hand.

'I should leave you in peace, Captain Swiffen.'

'So soon? I've got to share this Cognac with someone, and rather you than my room-mate to whom you'll be leaving me to the mercy of, along with his wretched chess board. I can tell you in confidence, that 'crashing bore doesn't even begin to describe him adequately.'

Alex laughed slightly, emptying his glass; he offered Daniel his hand once again, only this time with insistence.

Daniel gazed at him, shaking his head. 'You're eager to take your leave I can tell, so I won't make you feel uneasy, by insisting that you have another Cognac, but I think we have gone beyond the point of just shaking hands don't you?'

Alex took a step backwards and Daniel put a reassuring hand on his arm. Alex opened his mouth to speak, but no words came out, his throat felt dry.

'It's ok. I felt a frisson of something the first time we met, at the CCS and I think you did as well. So we can acknowledge it, and leave it at that.'

Alex shrugged, holding his ground as Daniel edged forward and they embraced, like brothers or comrades in arms. Then he lent his head against Alex's forehead. 'Good luck Lance-Corporal. Stay safe if you can. I know your beloved Laura is waiting for you!'

Alex smiled. He could only have mentioned Laura to Daniel once before today, and yet he had remembered, while Eloise Chagal, had viewed his love for Laura as an irrelevance; someone far away, who was still standing between her and what she wanted, whereas Daniel, being the gentleman he was, despite how strong his feelings might have been, and Alex didn't doubt them for a moment, accepted Laura's place in his life without question.

They parted and Alex smiled. He offered his hand, which Daniel took, shaking it warmly. 'It's goodbye then,' Alex said and Daniel nodded, half turning, he made a point of doing something inconsequential, like tidying his belongings.

'I ask one last favour Lance-Corporal, that when I turn around I want you to have left.'

Alex nodded, turning sharply, he thought for a second about saying something inconsequential, but erred as he knew it wasn't what Daniel wanted. This time it would be goodbye and they will have parted as friends.

Only after he heard the click of the door, did Daniel turn around, taking a huge breath. In that brief moment of embrace – although he couldn't be sure whether Alex Conyer felt the same – he had come close to wanting to see what that frisson they both felt, actually amounted to, but he had pulled back, and not because he was particularly scared, but because he had to. In that drab cold claustrophobic cabin, he was left with the stark reality of reconciling himself to that was how it had to be.

London – November, 1916

Daniel Swiffen had been on leave three days and he already felt lethargic, lacking in purpose and direction. Rudderless as his father would describe it. He feared telling the Old Man about his referral to Craiglockhart Hospital as he suspected what opinion might be drawn, but Major Templar had been adamant that his attendance there would precede any return to the Front. He had pleaded with his CO for it not to be formerly added to his record, but the Major's hands had been tied and there was Lieutenant Sallis's court martial to consider.

He had returned home to Cavendish Square, having telegrammed ahead requesting Lavinia to meet him in London, and when he arrived, was shocked to see her in black.

'Who?'

'Andrew, two weeks ago.'

Daniel went white. Shaking slightly he offered her both his hands and squeezed hers. 'I'm truly sorry. When is the funeral?'

'Last week. I wasn't sure you would get leave at such short notice, or we could have delayed it. He's been interred in the churchyard close to the family home. He left you this.'

Lavinia took a letter from her bag, handing it to Daniel. 'I wish he could have avoided action on medical grounds. He was never equipped for it, emotionally. My parents are devastated of course. Their only son gone. A fate that many families are having to adjust to, as many more will yet, before this wretched war is over.'

Lavinia slumped into a chair and turned her face from Daniel's gaze. He laid a hand on her shoulder, squeezing gently as he expected her to weep, but no tears came.

'I was thinking of going to the convalescent home where Martin is being treated but I can postpone if you want us to return to Javrons together?'

Lavinia shook her head slowly. He meant well, she knew, but she couldn't cope with him being considerate. 'No. You go as you planned. How long is your leave?'

'Three weeks at home followed by another two weeks at Craiglockhart Hospital for physiological assessment.'

Lavinia turned sharply. 'Why?'

'Because Major Templar is convinced that I need it before returning to action. Not normal conduct apparently, putting a revolver against your Lieutenant's chin and threatening to blow his bloody brains out. Even if he is an intolerable shit!'

Lavinia could tell despite the ironic, casual tone that he wasn't jesting. 'Why would you do that?'

'Because Sallis was an interloper, a menace. Quite possibly a seditionist who incited raw young recruits to desert without a care that if caught they would face a firing squad and all apparently in the cause of the ordinary "working man".

Lavinia attempted to stand up, but her legs were wobbly so she sat back down, but when Daniel tried to placate her, with a gentle hand on her shoulder, she shrugged it away, sighing heavily.

'I no longer have the capacity to be surprised by anything you do Daniel. In fact I'm not sure I even know you anymore.'

Daniel nodded slowly. 'So now I have this blasted war to thank for the fact that I'm now a stranger to my own wife?'

'No Daniel. You have your own actions to blame for that. You confess to wanting to kill a fellow officer in cold blood and express no shame or remorse.'

'Remorse, for the likes of Sallis? If you met the man, you wouldn't think him worthy of your sympathy. I can only imagine how he would have treated someone of Andrew's emotional vulnerability. The man is a bully. It's ironic actually, that I told the Major that if I had ordered Sallis to go "over the top" into No Man's Land, in the hope that there might be an enemy sniper's bullet intended for him, and I wouldn't even be sorry, but that would be ok, according to the conventional Rules of Engagement in warfare.'

Lavinia stood up this time and looked Daniel squarely in the eye. 'Rationalise this however you wish, because I'm past caring. Go to visit Martin Fearns. I shall return to Javrons alone when I'm ready. Now if you will excuse me, I'm going to rest, as I'm still grieving for my brother! Read Andrew's letter. I daresay it will be an affectionate one!'

Lavinia left the room without another word or even a backward glance. He found he couldn't even react to her comment about Andrew's letter as she had said it, so matter-of-factly, without any emotion. Yes she was bound to still be grieving and what he had told her, hadn't helped. Yet all the progress he felt they had made on his last leave had evaporated.

While her remark about being past caring was, he knew, as significant a verdict on the state of their marriage, as all the anger she had previously succumbed to ever would be.

Convalescent Hospital– Oxfordshire.

Daniel arrived around midday, with a bottle of Martin Fearns' favourite Cognac. Dressed in civilian clothes, he tried to appear relaxed, urbane, although it was the furthest from what he felt. A middle-aged nurse took him out into the manicured gardens, to where Martin was sat, in his chair with a tartan rug across his knees, keeping out a November chill, only mildly offset by weak winter sunshine.

Daniel had taken considerable effort to school himself not to be shocked by the sight of Martin's injuries. The livid facial scar, which his best man had been told might fade with time, and the useless dead weight of his right arm, which with continued physiotherapy might be partially usable. Might. A term which men like Martin had been forced to come to terms with.

'Captain Swiffen!' he said with what sounded like forced joviality, but Daniel knew Martin was pleased to see him. He lightly shook his left hand, sitting in the wicker chair, an orderly had provided.

'They grant you some precious leave and you waste it on visiting me? Very decent of you!'

'Spend on you Martin. Not waste. Never that. What's all this Captain Swiffen business. I am on leave, you're invalided out. It's Daniel!'

He showed Martin the bottle of Cognac, surreptitiously with a sly wink. 'I trust you'll be allowed this. I smuggled it in somehow.'

Daniel had been determined on the train journey to avoid

the usual platitudes and not to ask Martin how he was, as it must be blatantly obvious, but now he was here, he had gone dry. Reading Andrew's letter again before setting off hadn't helped, and Lavinia had been right. It was an affectionate one. To the very last Andrew Restarick hadn't reconciled himself to what his sexuality meant and the dangers it represented. He had confessed to loving Daniel as much as he had when they had been at Eton. Although he had stressed that he regretted putting them both at risk by acting upon it. He could never regret feeling it, and he had explained to Daniel that the opposition to his marrying Lavinia was because he had known his sister would feel betrayed by their past, and because he was consumed with jealousy. Daniel had read the letter three times the previous night over a Cognac, and its contents had dogged him throughout his journey here.

When he awoke that morning, his valet had informed him that Lavinia had made good on her vow to return alone to Javrons that morning. He freely admitted that coming here was as much about making himself feel better as it was about lifting Martin's spirits. He was tired of being portrayed the bad guy, or simply misunderstood. He had to make amends and coming here was a start.

'So, how's things?' asked Martin after a brief silence. He had always been intuitive so Daniel couldn't lie.

'Andrew Restarick didn't make it. Shot at Mametz. He left me a letter, which he hadn't dated.'

'I'm so sorry. How's Lavinia taken it?'

'She's distraught. Very angry. Disillusioned!'

'With the war? That's understandable.'

'Yes, but not only with the war. With me and the state of our marriage. The fact that her brother, believed he was infatuated with me to the last.'

'Oh!' said Martin, his tone as neutral as he could manage.

'Yes she knows. After the ceremony Andrew came to my

suite, confronted me about how I had duped Lavinia into marriage. Dazzled her with the trappings of my title, the estate, etc, etc, even after he had done everything to discourage her. Lavinia overheard us. Now he's written this letter, confessing he had been motivated by jealousy.'

Martin shook his head slowly, as Daniel lit them both a cigarette, putting one between Martin's lips despite his protests.

'Poor Restarick. He never did understand the risks he was taking by, being so open about his feelings.'

Daniel shrugged. 'I think he understood, I'm not sure whether he cared enough. Lavinia said she wished he had qualified for medical exemption as he was never equipped emotionally to cope with fighting and it would appear that she was right. I can't imagine how he would have coped with prison as that's where he'd end up had the likes of Frobisher or Crowley ever discovered us together.'

Martin drew heavily on his cigarette, and looking at Daniel, he was puzzled. 'It's a damn good job you were stronger, emotionally speaking, as you resisted temptation with Trentham's guidance when it was required.'

Daniel smiled and his mind flashed back to the day that he and Martin had visited the CCS and they were led into the wrong marquee and met Private Alex Conyer as he then was; the young Devonshire recruit, whose name had been similar to one of their own battalion's wounded. He had experienced that strange reaction to him, just as he had recently on the troop ship home, and he had wondered now if Martin had misread any sign in his reaction.

'At least you were never tempted after Eton, although I can't help wondering if poor Restarick was.'

Daniel inhaled the last drag on his cigarette and then stubbed it into the grass under his feet. Martin laughed. 'Don't let the Matron catch you doing that. They take enormous pride in the perfect condition of the lawns and they have a dim view of smoking. Which as you can see is widely ignored.'

'It looks a well-run place.'

'It's hell Daniel. Then the trenches were hell and hearing of Restarick's fate reminds me that despite this…' Martin flicked the sleeve of his right arm and pointed to his facial scar, '…I'm still one of the lucky ones.'

Daniel smiled, tapping Martin gently on the shoulder, and soon they fell into a companionable reminiscence of happier times, before the war blighted every hope, every dream they had cultivated. Days, the likes of which they would never see again. On the journey back to London, Daniel began to understand that Martin Fearns was a credit to himself and his family, and that for him there was nothing to be gained by becoming a hostage to his own self-pity.

Craiglockhart Hospital – January, 1917

The doctor looked out of the window as golfers started their game. At a guess he would have expected his current patient to be a golfer, but apparently he wasn't – a salient lesson he thought that a man of his professional experience shouldn't rush to assumptions. He checked the time and replaced his pocket watch, before turning towards his patient.

Captain Swiffen was nonetheless a very complex man. Resisting the urge to be flattered by his hereditary status, he had been waiting for the chance to interview him for weeks. He wanted to know as much as he could about what motivated this man, but he guessed he would have to tread softly. He was supposed to be seeing Dr Rivers, but he had been assigned to him at the last minute – for this session at least – and Copeland was determined to make the most of the opportunity.

Steepling his fingers, he pondered how to approach the

difficult subject and he decided on being direct. He could always ease back later if the patient appeared reticent or worse aggressive.

'Tell me Captain Swiffen, what were your intentions when you pressed your revolver against Lieutenant Sallis's chin?' The question was asked plainly in a flat neutral tone, without a trace of inflection or nuance, and Daniel smiled. He had been informed that Dr Rivers was one of the top men here and he could expect to be seeing him, but this chap Copeland was good. He had grown up being used to the direct approach, but in adulthood his title, motivated deference, in some, cloying sycophancy in others, but Copeland was inclined to neither. He wanted the facts and he wanted them straight.

Daniel smiled, reaching for his cigarette case, he opened it. 'May I?'

Copeland nodded. His smile was serene. Patience personified. What would it take to rile a man like Copeland? Daniel wondered, as he lit the cigarette. A lot more than it had taken to rile Sallis that was for sure.

'My first inclination was to blow his bloody brains out! We had received intelligence, you see that he had incited at least two recruits to desert. Actively encouraged them. There was an acceptance, that those caught in the act of deserting were inclined to say anything that would save them from the firing squad, but during interrogation they adhered stubbornly to their version of events. Asserting that they had only deserted when gently coerced by Sallis, even though they were offered no suggestion of reprieve. I admit, that I had personal issues with Lieutenant Sallis – or to be accurate –he had issues with me, largely due to class prejudice. I became convinced that he was politically motivated to incite those vulnerable men to desert. It was an incitement to treason.'

'It would have been hard to prove a case against Lieutenant Sallis though wouldn't it? Might it be suggested you acted rashly, that you wanted him to face summary justice of your own choosing?'

Daniel finished his cigarette and stubbing it out he looked directly at Copeland and said, 'That's an interesting distinction you make. Because my CO, Major Templar, was blunt. He called it attempted murder!'

Dr Copeland half smiled. Daniel recognised it as the smile of a man who was totally neutral. He offered no opinion either way. 'You'll continue?' he prompted Daniel, who shrugged. He contemplated lighting another cigarette, but hesitated, wondering if Copeland would leap to conclusions about that as well. 'Major Templar didn't place you under arrest though did he?'

'No, he arrested Sallis instead. Although I was taken out of action immediately which was a huge sacrifice for the battalion, but the Major was unequivocal. It was leave and then referral here, to Craiglockhart, which he inferred was non-negotiable. He couldn't wait to get the paperwork sorted and me on the next troop ship home.'

'He saved your skin in effect?'

Daniel nodded, this time he reached for the cigarette case lighting one, regardless of what Copeland implied from it.

'Indeed. I think it's fair to say that initially I did resent Lieutenant Sallis, for reasons he couldn't possibly be responsible for, which I accept was unjust, irrational even, however, I had been very close to Lieutenant Fearns, his predecessor, who was best man at my wedding. So naturally the relationship wasn't the same. The understanding, the instinct to rely upon, didn't exist but Sallis also resented me, I discovered quickly for reasons, I had no control over: like position, class, a tradition of birthright I had inherited, a privileged upbringing which he utterly despised. All of that aside, he chose to act as he did, he consciously told those recruits that they should desert if they wanted to, that he would look the other way, safe in the knowledge that all the risk was theirs, and they would be punished if caught. So he got what he deserved.'

'The butt of your revolver?'

'No that was my error. One I cannot go back and undo. I was referring to the court-martial. There was something else he said, that some might see as mitigation, for my behaviour, which I never mentioned to the Major, but Sallis whispered into my ear, that he would expect me to look after the new recruits, because that's what my class always did...' Daniel paused mimicking the quotation marks, with his fingers, adding, '...at Eton. We looked after our boys!'

Copeland who had been scribbling notes looked up at that moment, his brows pleated in a deep frown.

'Do you have any idea what he was implying by the term "our boys"?'

Daniel smiled. Either Copeland had led a very sheltered life or he was just being politely obtuse, which was intriguing as he didn't come across as the sycophantic type.

'Oh yes doctor, it was implicit in every syllable he uttered. Insidious, imbued with all the class ridden resentment that rose like bile from Lieutenant Sallis's throat. He was implying that I was homosexual!'

Copeland coughed and Daniel suppressed a smile. 'Why would he believe that?'

'Because it fitted his preconceptions. despite knowing I was married. You see, where men like Sallis are concerned, the facts are irrelevant. I daresay he might have met another Etonian whose privileged background had rankled with him, and whose sexuality might have been more ambiguous. So for a man of Sallis's prejudices we all had to be so inclined.'

Dr Copeland bowed his head slightly, completing his notes, while Daniel drew heavily on his cigarette, creating a cloud of blue-grey smoke around him. He expected Copeland would be reticent about asking directly whether there was any truth in Sallis's accusation, but he couldn't resist speculating on whether he would probe, however opaquely, into what Stephen Trentham had always referred to as his "proclivities."

Although he realised that had he expected to see shock in Copeland's expression, then he was destined to be disappointed. Daniel had no concern about Sallis's insinuation regarding his sexuality, going any further than Copeland's files, and he left the interview with a lot to intrigue him, although he later acknowledged to himself concern that it might develop into a recurring theme for Copeland at future sessions, but this also proved groundless. Whether Copeland thought it was irrelevant, or that he had concluded that it was an imagined prejudice on Daniel's part, remained unexplored. For himself though, Daniel had become convinced that Copeland had reached the conclusion from examination that he relied upon the concept of Sallis's prejudice against him as sufficient motive for all that had taken place between them, rather than accepting that they simply couldn't abide each other, as so often occurred in all walks of life. He also inferred in another session that Daniel's actions couldn't be easily explained by him suffering from psychosis or shellshock as so many of the cases admitted to Craiglockhart were. It could be down to combat fatigue, or the burden of command, Copeland had acknowledged, to which Daniel had detected the doubt in his tone, even at these suggestions, but pure rage compelled Daniel to act as he had in Copeland's view, and to these lengths he was fortunate to have escaped serious punishment.

'So my being sent here was a soft option in your view? A box-ticking exercise enabling Major Templar to have me back at the Front, without fear that I might be tempted to put my revolver against another man's chin and threaten to blow their brains out, because they don't like which school I went to.'

Copeland opened his arms expansively and said, 'Perhaps.

Yes. I am convinced you're invaluable to him, and he wants to be sure he can convince the top brass that you are fit to return.'

'Do you resent me for the fact that I went to Eton, Dr Copeland? Or for the likelihood that one day I will inherit the Earldom of Royston, provided of course that I'm not so careless to get my head blown off, in what remains of this bloody war?'

Dr Copeland retained his calm demeanour. Steepling his fingers, he tapped them against his pursed lips, waiting for Daniel's ire to be calmed. Finally he spoke. 'Why should I? I have spoken to many men here, and my purpose has always been the same, to help them understand the trauma they have suffered, in warfare. Craiglockhart is a hospital for officers as you know Captain Swiffen, and we admit officers from all backgrounds.

'You are not the first titled son of the estate to be admitted and I doubt that you will be the last. I would like to have it said of me that I endeavour to see the patient, to assess their condition and to successfully treat it. Although it is out my hands that once assessed as fit we are consigning many of them back to the Front to suffer the same fate that brought them to us, in the first place, but I can assure you Captain Swiffen that I am not interested, or overly impressed by a preoccupation with old school ties.'

'Even so you still think I got off lightly, by being assigned here?'

Copeland fidgeted slightly, but Daniel didn't pick up on it as a sign. 'I firmly believe from what you have told me that you were extremely fortunate to have had Major Templar as your CO, but also for the fact that Lieutenant Sallis may be a seditionist! A traitor to his country. That does put a different complexion upon a man and the opinions that others have of him which perhaps adds more mitigation to the rashness of your actions, which in other circumstances is more than you might have deserved.'

Daniel fixed Copeland with a hard stare. He had been expecting to see Dr William Rivers, whose reputation according to Templar, reached beyond the confines of Craiglockhart, but he had heard rumours that Copeland was keen to continue with his treatment and had sought the approval of his colleagues to do so. But why? Daniel didn't consider himself to be so unique a case that the medical staff would be clamouring to interview him. Did Copeland strive for the opportunity to say all that he just had? That despite his assurances about not giving a jot about Old School Ties, he did in fact resent him as Sallis had, although not with the same level of vehemence?

Daniel's hand shook as he tried to light another cigarette and standing, Copeland finished the task for him, watching Daniel as he sat down, drawing heavily on the cigarette. Copeland checked his watch. 'We've had a particularly long session today, so you deserve your leisure time.'

Daniel mumbled his thanks as he stood. At the door, with his hand poised on the knob, he turned and said. 'I was led to believe I would be seeing Dr Rivers. Will that be possible next time?'

If Copeland was disappointed he was damned if he would show it, Daniel thought with a thin smile. 'If that is what you wish.'

'It is, thank you.'

Daniel left, convinced that while his request to see Dr Rivers for his next session would be acceded to, in the mind of a man like Dr Copeland the concession would only serve to prove that titled men like him usually did get what they wanted, and they perceived to be their due, in the end. He returned to his room quietly satisfied; this was a situation he could readily accept, but what surprised him more was the fact that he didn't give a damn whether the likes of Dr Copeland liked the situation or not.

15

Covington, Devon

Alex came home a changed man. He bore the scars of his experiences at the Front, with dignity but he wasn't yet inclined to share them.

As the Great Western train trundled into Covington he could see visible signs of change, but it was what he felt that unnerved him. Once, he would have seen Laura, her face flushed with happiness at his arrival, her green eyes dancing merrily as she waved from the scullery window, but not today. As he pushed open the door and stepped onto the platform, he half expected to see Stoughton approach and goad him with a barbed comment, and for George to blow his whistle as the train was ready to depart. An adolescent porter, like many of the volunteers who had lied about their age to enlist, stepped forward, but Alex could manage his luggage, so he gave the young man something for his trouble, as he waited for Laura to come running down the platform into his waiting arms.

He had wired from Paddington that he was coming today, so now her absence had him seriously worried. Striding down the platform,he smiled at a few faces that he recognised, but none seemed to acknowledge him as he looked older without his widow's peak.

He knocked gently on the back door of the station master's cottage and finding it open, stepped inside. 'Laura,' he shouted. There was an eeriness about the place he didn't recognise, although everything looked the same. Laura came downstairs and smiled at Alex. 'Hi lass, I thought you might have met me on the platform.' Laura smiled wanly. She pulled the telegram from her apron pocket as Alex looked around him. The slippers under the chair by the fire, then up at the mantelpiece, where George had kept his favourite pipe, and then finally the reality dawned on him. George was gone and yet Laura hadn't written him with her devastating news. But why?

He felt his throat go dry, but he knew she needed him to be strong for her. 'When?' is all he could manage.

'November last,' she said through half sobs and hiccups, and then as Alex opened his arms, she ran into his embrace and sobbed like she never had before.

Later that evening, they lay in bed and Alex held Laura to him, gently stroking her arm. 'Tell me what happened.'

'It was a heart attack. He just suddenly collapsed on the scullery floor. He had been arguing with Stoughton, who had forced his attentions on me, again, but I was handling it. Dad lashed the horsewhip at Stoughton drawing blood on his cheek, so Stoughton retaliated, pulling at the whip which sent Dad stumbling. At first I thought he had just lost his balance, but, I quickly saw that he couldn't speak, and he was clutching his left arm, so I knew how serious it was and I shrieked at Stoughton to get help.'

Alex looked at her, his face grim. Knowing there was more, he nodded, urging her to continue. 'They took him to the cottage hospital and they hoped to transfer him to Exeter Infirmary but he was just too weak. In the end I knew I had to let him go.'

Laura bit her bottom lip to stem the flow of tears from falling again as Alex held her tighter, closer. 'So what about this cottage? How come you've been allowed to stay?'

Laura gulped and he saw the faint trace of a smile cross her face. 'The management at Great Western have been fantastic. They valued Dad's long years of service so highly, and although they had to put someone in charge, they said I could stay here, until I found somewhere else. Then it transpired that the man they had found lived a couple of stations down the line, where he lived with his family and because he didn't want them uprooted I was given longer. I don't want to stay here long term. The place is too full of memories and while I can't let go yet, I will need to move on. We will need to move on.'

Alex kissed her forehead, nodding. 'So what happened to Stoughton?'

'That is the best news of all, because I feared they would put him in charge. It appeared, however, that any female, he took a fancy to was considered fair game. He made a nuisance of himself with any female passenger who caught his eye, until one day, he picked the wrong girl. It turned out that her father had considerable financial holding in Great Western and once she had reported Stoughton, the executives seized their chance to be rid. You know Dad always suspected he must have had an ally at Head Office, covering his back, well we were wrong. They were just waiting until they had enough 'dirt' on him that would stick and on which they could justify dismissal.'

'Was he to blame for George's death?'

Laura shook her head. 'As much as I would like to lay the blame at him, the doctors told me, Dad was at risk of a heart attack and it could have happened anytime. When it did, he just wasn't strong enough. I'm sorry I didn't write, but there was nothing you could do. I figured if you were there worrying about me grieving, it would be a distraction, and I needed you to focus on fighting and surviving so eventually you would come back to me, as you are all I have left now.'

Alex kissed her hard on the mouth, nodding. 'We both only have each other.'

'So you know about Effie?'

Alex nodded. 'One of my "duty" letters to her came back and a neighbour wrote to explain that she had passed.'

'I tried keeping in touch, so did Dad, but she never made it easy. After her last gentleman friend abandoned her she became more embittered, more cut off from everyone. I'm sorry.'

'Don't be. Sadly the gin bottle had been my mother's favourite companion for too long. While my grandfather was alive, he would try to keep her straight, but she never listened to me, when I was old and bold enough to try. She always said it wasn't my place and I guess she was right. None of her gentlemen friends ever cared enough or stayed long enough to encourage her to cut back, although I doubt she would have listened.'

Laura got out of bed and tiptoed to a large chest of draws, from which she unearthed the gold watch he had left with her for safe keeping. She dropped it into his outstretched palm. 'Back where it belongs.'

He ran his thumb across the engraving on his grand-father's watch. Now he bit back tears of his own. 'My last link with the past. I guess we both need to move on eventually and that's what we'll do Laura. Together.'

'For eternity.' She leaned into him, adding, 'But you're not thinking of selling it?'

Alex shook his head. 'I don't want to, but if needs must I would.'

Laura lay down again, leaning her head against his chest, and gripping his hand, she slept. When Alex was certain she was asleep, he eased out of bed pulling on his trousers and crept downstairs. In the dwindling light the cottage felt eerier than ever, but he pulled on his boots and headed out edging towards the town and the tiny church where he would one day very soon make his vow of commitment to Laura. He headed into the churchyard where an elderly gardener gave him directions to the stark wooden cross that marked George Weston's grave.

Fighting back tears that he didn't want to shed, he ran a hand along the top of the cross and let it rest there. Forcing the words past the lump in his throat, he said, 'I've come back for her George, as I promised I would, and I'll look after her, just as you strove to do all those years.' He angrily wiped aside the tears that had come unbidden, and continued, 'We'll get you a proper headstone as well in due course. A marble one as befits Covington's best ever station-master, and one of the best men I've ever known!'

He half turned brushing the last stray tears away, before heading back. The gardener stopped him at the gate. 'I'm so sorry son as I didn't recognise you at first. She's missed him so much has that lass. We all have. George Weston was part of the fabric of this town, and we look after our own.'

Alex nodded. 'Well she has no need to worry. She will always miss him and that's how it should be, but it's my job to look after her now!'

The gardener slapped Alex good naturedly on the shoulder and as he took his leave, walking back to the station-master's cottage, he thought back to those days before the war began, when Covington stifled him within the limits of its boundaries. That staying here also limited the scope of his imagination and ambition. For now he couldn't imagine being anywhere else. As he entered the cottage, Laura was at the range stirring a saucepan. She instructed him to sit, and half turning she said, 'Where did you go?'

'The graveyard. I wanted to say my goodbyes to George and to renew the promise I made to him, the night we spent together in the room above the Inn. That I would come back to you and look after you always, whether he was around to do so or not. So, because he isn't, I had to renew that promise.'

Alex kissed her then as he used to, and because she couldn't speak past the lump that had formed in her throat, she kissed his forehead. 'I miss your widow's peak. It was such a big part of you! Will you try growing it back?'

Alex smiled, shaking his head. 'No, because it was a feature of the boy that I was, who went off to fight a war, but it's not part of the man who has come back.'

Laura smiled as she ladled homemade broth into bowls and set them on the table. She still hadn't got accustomed to the fact that he was back and thankfully safe. Sitting down, she began slicing bread, her eyes fixed on him. For the first time since she had walked back alone from the cottage hospital the night her father died, she had begun to live again and to believe she could be happy once more and she had Alex to thank for that.

Later that night, Alex lay in bed with Laura next to him, curled into his warmth. She craved intimacy, but she respected that he wanted comfort. She gently pulled his left arm around her neck and lay cushioned against his right shoulder, their legs entwined. 'I've witnessed some horrific scenes the likes of which I never want to see again, but which cannot be unseen. One morning I woke and finding the man next to me was a corpse, I skewered a rat that was crawling up to make a meal of his face. I realised he must have perished from the cold in his sleep. You were right to be cautious I think, however difficult it was becoming, for me to avoid the war.'

'So, what now? Will you have to go back?'

'I'm not sure, I hope not. I could try for my old job at the *Echo*, but fear I might have outgrown that and it's certainly not my future. I remember saying how I felt Covington restrained me. You were here and that was what binded me to this town. Now having been away and seen what horrors, the world has the power to inflict, I'm no longer convinced that Covington's restrictive limits are so bad. I decided on the way home that we must get a headstone for George's grave. One that befits his status in Covington and what its people meant to him and what he was to them.'

Laura was crying now and she let the tears roll down her cheeks. She felt her father's loss very keenly everyday and she knew it would be that way for awhile. She had Alex back and that helped dissipate the burden of loss, but more importantly, she was grateful to be one of the lucky ones as many women of her generation hadn't been as fortunate. The pain of losing a husband or a son was etched deep into the faces of many in towns and cities across the country and for some she knew, it still wasn't over. The legacy of this wretched war was visible everywhere you looked. For herself she still wasn't convinced it had been a price worth paying, although she kept her own counsel, not wanting to be viewed as unpatriotic while the war still had to be won.

So much had changed since the first volunteers had marched with hope in their hearts and with the crowds' cheers ringing in their ears in the bright glorious sunlight of summer three years ago. With it, had been all the optimism of an early victory that was just a fading memory now. She would let Alex relive his experiences of life at the Front when he was ready, and if that time didn't come for months or even years, then she would keep her counsel there also. Grateful that he wanted to spare her. All she had now was Alex Conyer, and their love which had remained strong despite the ravages of war that had threatened to tear them apart. A love that could sustain them for the rest of their days and she was grateful that, for her, there had been a reprieve.

The Javrons Estate, Hertfordshire– Winter, 1917

The first snows of winter had come to the estate and the lawn edging the sweeping gravel drive, was a blanket of startling white, while icicles hung in the trees. The drawing room felt eerie in the pervading silence as the confirmation they had been dreading came in a telegram, three days before Lavinia, the Viscountess Swiffen, was due to mark her third wedding anniversary. The footman had handed the telegram to the Earl on a silver salver, and the Earl ripped it open, dismissing his staff with a brisk nod. He read the contents and then gripping the mantel-piece, for support he took a long deep breath to compose himself, before handing it to Lavinia. The pain constricting his chest was vice-like in its intensity and although he had once scathingly predicted his son would die in his first few weeks at the Front, he had never prepared himself for the reality of his grief.

The contents of the telegram had been stark. Captain Daniel Swiffen, of the Hertfordshire Regiment had been killed in action late October 1917 in the offensive to secure the ridge at Ypres, close to the tiny Belgian village of Passchendaele.

The Earl reached for his wife's hand, squeezing it tight as the Countess Swiffen closed her eyes, reciting her own prayers. The issue of their only son volunteering for war had been a contentious one between them as the Countess always feared Daniel wouldn't cope. 'Our son is a poet not a soldier. Never a soldier,' although she had never quite reconciled herself to the fact that other aspiring poets had also heeded the call to arms. While for the Earl it had always been about duty. The Swiffens had a proud history of doing theirs so if the regiment called him he would expect him to heed the call. 'Damn the bloody regiment!' had been the Countess's response in one of the rare moments that she hadn't felt obliged to stand solidly by her husband's view. Elizabeth Swiffen had no idea how she was going to cope with her grief, but it would be endured with dignity as she took her daughter-in-law's hand, and held it tight.

It had been on Daniel's last leave, after his time at Craiglockhart Hospital ended and he was about to return to action, that they finally managed to conceive a child, due in February.

Retrieving the telegram, she re-read it again, trying to absorb the facts that she was a widow and couldn't help thinking what a colossal waste it was. Just as she had when her beloved brother, Andrew had perished, as she had always had doubts that he was emotionally equipped to fight a war as the Countess had been about Daniel.

The battle for Passchendaele, had raged on for months since July, Daniel had written her about how the regiment had been decimated on the first day, and the carnage had continued through the unimaginable mud and rain of autumn as the slaughter continued. The Earl took some solace in that his son had played his part in another crucial stage of the war.

He hadn't wanted to return to the Front, after Craiglockhart, Lavinia had been certain of that, and his later letters had shown his mood at its bleakest. There had been subtle changes in him after Craiglockhart and his analysis with the psychologists. Lavinia had been forced to revaluate her opinion of her husband after he had relayed the incident involving Lieutenant Sallis, and she also believed Daniel had genuinely grieved for the loss of her brother Andrew, even though she had been cruelly dismissive.

Their marriage had entered what now turned out to be its final stage and she had done her duty by him with a child. It had to be a boy for the means to have justified the end, along with all the pain and anguish they had put each other through to get there.

Daniel had struggled at Craiglockhart. The subsequent sessions with Dr William Rivers had forced to him analyse exactly what his true feelings were for Lavinia, for Andrew Restarick, and Alex Conyer, who he had never met more than twice. Although self-analysis was never something a man of his background and class would normally indulge in, he felt able by the time of his discharge to acknowledge the benefits of therapy. So prior to leaving the safe confines of Craiglockhart and his return to action he had written Lavinia a letter, with the strict instructions that it should only be opened in the event of his death.

She read it that night in the privacy of her bedroom suite, and although its contents were startling, she knew Daniel no longer held the ability to surprise her. That in so many ways, he and Andrew had been so alike. He stated that he wished he could have loved her in the manner a man should love his wife, but although he had tried his best, it just hadn't been in him. He confirmed she had been right, just as Andrew had been right, that her brother would always hold a place in his affections, that she could never claim, and would probably never understand. She smiled at this line, because the irony was, she did understand, because she had always understood her brother.

She stood by the fire in her silk nightdress stretched taut across the swell of her stomach. She ran a hand over it, feeling the baby kick. She bent down onto the chaise lounge and dropped the letter into the fire, watching the bright orange flames consume it. Consigning her dead husband's confession to ashes.

Major Templar had indicated that it was likely Daniel would receive a posthumous DSO for his outstanding courage in battle at Passchendaele. This caused her to smile as outstanding courage in battle was the least Daniel had ever expected himself capable of. Her father-in-law had also indicated that there would be a memorial service for Daniel at the local church. Lavinia would do her duty and participate in them all. For her now, all that mattered was the child growing inside her. Motherhood would become the focus of her energies, and she could only hope that it would be the long hoped for son, whose birth would continue the long unbroken line of succession, that the Swiffens had enjoyed for generations and, in the years to come, loved and cherished, the next Viscount Swiffen would fare better, and be happier than his father ever was.

POSTSCRIPT

A century has passed now since that first Armistice, when at the eleventh hour, beneath the pewter grey sky of a November day, the guns fell silent, bringing to an end, the most catastrophic conflict that the human race had thus far, inflicted upon itself. A war to end all war.

In the years since, an ongoing pilgrimage has come to the sites of special significance. Paying respect to long lost descendants, who in many cases they never met, but whose tales of heroism and sacrifice have been passed down through generations. Their final resting place marked by a white headstone bearing the name of a father, brother, husband, lover, or a son. Row upon row of identical headstones against verdant fields, suffused with scarlet poppies growing stiffly in the breeze.

In the distance on Thiepval Ridge they can see the towering arch designed by Sir Edwin Lutyens, dedicated to the dead of the Somme. Here too they have gathered to pay tribute, eyes moist with tears, as they seek the names of their loved ones, carved into the stone of the monument. As the flags are lowered in the dwindling light of day, a lone bugler plays the Last Post and heads are bowed in memory of all the brave young men who went to fight the good fight and never came home. *At the going down of the sun, and in the morning, we will remember them.*

SELECT BIBLIOGRAPHY

Tim Butcher, *The Trigger: The hunt for Gavrilo Princip*: Vintage Books, 2015.

Greg King & Sue Woolmans, The Assassination of the Archduke: Macmillan, 2013.

Colin Clifford, *The Asquiths*: John Murray, 2003.

Pat Barker, *Regeneration*: Viking Penguin Books, 1991.

ACKNOWLEDGEMENTS

Firstly I would like to thank the staff at Crawley Library for their assistance in finding most of the titles listed in my Select Bibliography.

I am grateful also to the Royal British Legion for granting permission to quote a line from the poem: "The Fallen" by Laurence Binyon in the postscript to this novel.

Lastly, I would like to thank family and friends for, expressing as much interest in this, as they did in my previous book.

Although this is a work of fiction and the characters contained herein are a product of the author's imagination, they are I hope a reflection of the thousands of real heroes who heeded the call to arms. As in this centenary year of the Armistice, their sacrifice remains especially poignant.